DARK SECRET

Jenna Lister

Chivers Press • **G.K. Hall & Co.**
Bath, England **Thorndike, Maine USA**

This Large Print edition is published by Chivers Press, England, and by G.K. Hall & Co., USA.

Published in 2001 in the U.K. by arrangement with Robert Hale Limited.

Published in 2001 in the U.S. by arrangement with Robert Hale Limited.

U.K. Hardcover   ISBN 0-7540-4391-6   (Chivers Large Print)
U.K. Softcover   ISBN 0-7540-4392-4   (Camden Large Print)
U.S. Softcover   ISBN 0-7838-9332-9   (Nightingale Series Edition)

The text of this Large Print edition is unabridged.
Other aspects of the book may vary from the original edition.

Set in 16 pt. New Times Roman.

Printed in Great Britain on acid-free paper.

British Library Cataloguing in Publication Data available

Library of Congress Cataloging-in-Publication Data

Lister, Jenna.
      Dark secret / Jenna Lister.
          p.   cm.
      ISBN 0-7838-9332-9 (lg. print : sc : alk. paper)
      1. Scotland—Fiction. I. Title.
PR6062.I797 D37   2001
823'.914 21; aa05 10-13—dc00   00–049887

CHAPTER ONE

Vicky watched as the two identical coffins were lowered into the dark earth. She felt as if part of her, the essential part, was also being buried with the two people she loved best in all the world.

It was a warm, sunny spring day and the little Cornish churchyard was full of the brightness of daffodils. Pink blossom crowded the ornamental cherry trees and birds chirruped and sang as they made nests and declared their territory. It was a day full of new life and it seemed indecent somehow to Vicky. It should have been raining, like the tears she had shed, or cold, like the bleakness in her heart, not brimming with light and life.

She was uncomfortably warm in the black woollen dress. It hadn't been a good choice. She had bought it hurriedly and uncaring of her appearance. It was too large for one thing and swamped her slender, almost boyish figure. The drab blackness drained all the colour from her face and left her with a pallor that made the sprinkling of freckles on her nose and cheeks stand out in sharp relief. She had pulled her thick chestnut hair back from her face and fastened it with a black velvet bow.

She winced as the first spadeful of earth hit

the pale gold wood and a strangled sob broke from her lips.

'Come, my dear,' said the minister gently, 'there's nothing more you can do.' Vicky looked up, her vivid blue eyes drowning in a fresh wave of tears, and her gaze met that of a tall, dark man standing on the fringe of the little group of people who had come to her parents' funeral. He looked uncomfortable and out of place. He was dressed very correctly in a charcoal-grey suit, with a white shirt and black tie, but he didn't belong there. She didn't know him.

She glanced round the rest of the group assembled at the graveside. There weren't many people, neither of her parents had any immediate family and they had gathered few friends around them, preferring to remain in the self-contained little unit they had made for the three of them. They had been so happy together they had needed no-one else. There were just a few friends from the village, people like the doctor and his wife, the licensee of the local inn, the postmaster and some representatives from the art world. Some she had met, others she had heard of, but she couldn't put a name to the dark man.

The family solicitor was there and she realised that the man was with him, as they fell into step together, when the little party started to wend its way from the graveside.

Vicky got into the funeral car, thinking she

2

would have preferred to walk home, it was no distance from the churchyard. The vicar and his wife travelled with her, so that she would not be alone. They had been very kind to her, helping to make all the necessary arrangements after the accident. Vicky had been in a sort of numb limbo and had agreed to anything that was suggested to her with weary resignation. She didn't care what was done with the mortal remains of her mother and father, nothing could alter the fact that they were lost to her forever.

The car stopped outside the pink-washed house, overlooking the harbour, that had been home to Vicky all her life. They were the first to arrive, the rest of the mourners were sharing cars or walking. Mrs Mead, who had been coming in to clean for the Tremaynes for a number of years, had prepared refreshments and Vicky forced herself to go and see if everything was ready.

She opened the door to the bright, sunny sitting-room and cast an eye over the circular table that had been spread with a white linen table-cloth and covered with plates of sandwiches and delicacies. Vicky would be relieved when this part of it was over, too. Eating after a funeral seemed indecent, too, somehow, like having a party, but she recognised that it was expected, Cornish hospitality being what it was.

Mrs Mead heard her and bustled in. 'How

are you, Miss Vicky? Are the others on their way? Shall I put the kettle on to make tea?'

'I'm okay, Mrs Mead, I suppose. I shall be glad when today is over. Yes, put the kettle on.'

Mrs Drew, the minister's wife, patted Vicky's shoulder. 'You've borne up wonderfully well, dear, but I expect you could do with a cup of tea. I'll see if I can help Mrs Mead.'

The first arrivals were just straggling in, amongst them Edward Frost, her father's solicitor, and the strange dark man. The stranger seemed reticent about entering and Vicky found herself watching him. His face was too strongly boned to be handsome in the conventional sense, all angles and planes, but he was attractive and arresting. His hair was thick and black, with a tendency to wave. He was tall and muscled, but with no spare flesh. He must be about thirty, Vicky thought.

As if aware of her scrutiny, he suddenly looked straight into her eyes. His were storm-grey and they looked cold and troubled. They reminded Vicky of storm-tossed Cornish seas and she shuddered. She had good reason to be afraid of those seas.

Edward Frost spoke to her. 'Victoria, my dear, may I introduce Ross Cameron—he's a relative of your father.' Vicky's eyes widened. 'I didn't realise Daddy had any relatives, he never mentioned anyone.'

4

'I don't suppose he would,' murmured Ross Cameron, with a bitter note marring his otherwise attractive voice, with its faint trace of a Scottish accent. 'But the fact remains, I'm your . . .'

Before he could finish his sentence, Edward Frost had interrupted with a firm, 'Ross, not now, please. Leave it until later when everyone else has gone. I think Victoria has had enough to put up with this afternoon.'

Ross Cameron coloured slightly and said, 'I'm sorry, you're quite right. Hello, Victoria, I'm dreadfully sorry about your parents' deaths.' He held out a large hand and she slipped her slender one into it. He covered her hand with his free one and held hers in both of his hands for a few seconds.

Vicky felt her pulse quicken and was surprised; she had thought she was incapable of feeling any sort of emotion at the moment, but this man appeared to have triggered a response somehow.

They moved into the long sitting-room, which ran the length of the house, and Vicky found herself caught up with accepting condolences and offers of help from various people for the next hour. She would not risk having anything to eat, she felt she would choke on it, but she was grateful for the cup of tea that Mrs Drew pushed into her hand.

Eventually people began to dwindle away and Vicky started to collect up the dirty crockery. 'Leave that, Miss Vicky, I'll see to it,' said Mrs Mead firmly.

'Victoria, is there somewhere we could talk privately. I'm afraid I have to acquaint you with the terms of your father's will,' Edward Frost said apologetically.

'Today?' asked Vicky in surprise. 'Couldn't it wait a day or two?'

'I'm sorry, but I think not. Ross has travelled down from Scotland and I don't think he wants to linger down here too long. You see the will concerns him.'

Vicky felt amazement and the first stirrings of alarm. There was something odd about all this. Why would someone she had never heard of be involved in her father's will?

She nodded. 'Very well, but can I change first? I'm so hot and uncomfortable in this dress.'

'Of course, my dear, where would you like us to wait?' asked Edward.

'In the little study across the hall. I think there's some whisky in there, if you want something stronger than tea.'

She walked slowly up the stairs, her hand trailing over the shiny polished wood of the banister. Her room looked just as it had always looked—a young girl's room, with floral cotton bedspread and curtains to match, which fluttered in the breeze from the open window. Topsy, her large rag doll, that had been a present for her seventh birthday, sat on the window-ledge. Shelves were crammed with books and bric-a-brac that she had collected during her seventeen years.

Just over a week ago she'd been a carefree girl, full of plans for the future. Now she felt like a woman, with a burden of sorrow in her heart and the fear of an uncertain future overshadowing her. She had never had to cope with any problems on her own, her parents had cocooned her; now she had no-one close to turn to. Oh, people were kind, but they had their own lives to lead and families to care for, they didn't really want to be burdened with an orphaned teenager.

She dragged off the hateful black dress and swore she would never wear it again. She went over to the wash-basin and rinsed her face and arms, relishing the coolness of the water against her heated skin. Then she found a soft, full grey skirt and a white silk blouse and slipped them on. She looked at herself in the mirror and decided that she certainly looked better than in the black dress. There was more colour in her cheeks, but she looked younger than her years. She wondered if she should put on some make-up, but in the end decided against it. She left her hair fastened back, at least it was cool that way, and made her way downstairs.

When she reached the study, she paused with her hand on the knob of the door; she could hear the murmur of voices from within, but could not make out what was being said. She opened the door and walked in and they immediately stopped talking. The thought crossed her mind that they had been talking about her.

Edward Frost was sitting at her father's desk with some papers spread in front of him. Ross Cameron was sitting in a rather battered leather swivel-chair, that her mother had tried for years to get rid of but which her father had insisted on keeping, with his long legs stretched out. He swivelled the chair and watched her as she walked into the room. He smiled, and Vicky realised that it was the first time she had seen him smile. It was a very attractive smile and he said, 'Feel better? You certainly look better.'

Vicky blushed. She must have looked a real mess before.

'We took you at your word, Victoria, and helped ourselves. Hope that's all right.' Edward Frost indicated their whisky tumblers.

'Yes, of course.' Vicky sat nervously on the edge of a chair at the opposite corner of the desk to where Ross was sitting.

The solicitor cleared his throat. He seemed nervous and ill at ease and this surprised Vicky. She thought solicitors were always in complete control of the situation. He started to speak, pausing between his words as if wondering how best to break some news that he'd rather not.

'Victoria, this is rather a difficult job for me, having known you and your parents for many years. I feel I must tell you something of the background before I break what I'm sure will be some rather staggering news to you. I don't quite know where to begin. Much of your father's past is shrouded in mystery and was completely unknown to me until I read a letter that he enclosed with his will. You will probably be wondering who Ross is and why he should be here at such a time, when you have never heard of him before.'

Ross's face had been growing grimmer as Edward Frost meandered through these vague hints. Now he suddenly burst in with, 'For God's sake, Frost, why don't you just tell her. She's got to know. Skating round it like that isn't helping the situation.'

Vicky looked from one man to the other and an icy hand clutched at her heart. What horrible news had she to be told, that Edward Frost couldn't bring himself to say it?

'Know what? For goodness' sake one of you tell me, then.' She fixed her eyes on Ross, realising that he was more likely to say whatever had to be said, quickly.

'That your father was also my father. That I'm your half-brother,' he ground out, in a harsh unnatural voice.

Vicky felt as if someone had hit her hard in her ribs. She tried to find her voice, but no sound came. Then she tried again and

9

managed to whisper, 'I don't understand, why did he never say? Did my mother know?'

Ross said slowly and bitterly, 'I shouldn't think so. I don't suppose he wanted to broadcast his dark secret. I can't think why he's revealed it now, except that he appears to want me to be responsible for you.'

Ross's words pounded round in her head. She couldn't seem to take it in. Nothing seemed to make sense. That her father had had a child whom he had never acknowledged, that in fact this attractive man was her half-brother, none of it made sense. The strain of the day, the stress she had been under since the dreadful accident and now this unbelievable revelation, were too much for Vicky. The room started to tilt and revolve, everything went black and she felt herself slipping from her chair.

When she resurfaced it was to find herself supported by Ross Cameron's arm, his hand holding a glass of brandy to her lips and his voice saying gently, 'Drink this, there's a good girl.' She coughed as the raw spirits hit the back of her throat, and struggled to sit up. She was lying on the comfortable old chesterfield, another of her father's cherished pieces of furniture. 'Lie still a moment, until you're feeling better,' Ross said.

Edward Frost's voice broke in coldly. 'Perhaps if you'd left me to break the news gently, as I intended, that wouldn't have happened, young man. Have you any idea of the strain this poor child has been under?'

'Yes, I'm very sorry. You're quite right. How are you feeling now, Vicky?' Ross's voice was gentle and apologetic, the animosity had disappeared.

Vicky struggled into a sitting position, but couldn't swing her legs off the chesterfield because Ross was sitting there and made no move to get up.

Edward Frost got up from his chair and came towards her, a white envelope in his hand. 'Perhaps I'd better give you this first. I have no knowledge of its contents. I was merely instructed to hand it to you, should it be necessary to put into effect the provisions your father had made against anything happening to him and your mother before you came of age. He may have explained the circumstances to you.'

Vicky took the letter from him with fingers that shook slightly and there was complete silence as she withdrew the sheet of notepaper and read it.

'My darling Vicky. It is my fervent hope that you will never have to read this letter, for if you do it will mean that your mother and I have died before you reach adulthood. I want you to trust me and not judge, for there are circumstances that I still cannot explain to you without injuring another

11

party, but one day all will be revealed to you and to Ross, who must be confused and perhaps angry. You will, no doubt, hear that I left my wife Helen Cameron with an unborn child and that she subsequently committed suicide. It was a tragedy I regretted, but I could not have prevented it, please believe that.

'I have left all I possess to you, dearest child, but it may not be sufficient to keep you until such time as you are earning or marry and I realise that because of the manner in which your mother and I have sheltered you, you are probably ill-equipped to fend for yourself. I am, therefore, appointing Ross Cameron as your guardian, until you are twenty-one. The Camerons are in a position to help you and I feel they owe me something.

'Remember me as you have always known me. Please don't let people change your opinion of me. Trust me. Your devoted father.'

Vicky shook her head, still confused, and looked with troubled eyes first at Ross and then at Edward Frost. 'I still don't really understand. He says he left his wife, presumably your mother, Ross, with an unborn child, you, but he doesn't say why and he has apparently made you my guardian and seems to think you owe him something. It's all too

12

confusing for me.'

Edward Frost broke in at this juncture. 'Perhaps I could explain some of the circumstances to you, since you don't even know who the Camerons are. Ross's grandfather is Sir Malcolm Cameron and he was the father of the Helen Cameron your father married, Vicky. Your father had been commissioned to sculpt a bust of Helen for Sir Malcolm. She was his only child and he doted on her, mainly because his wife had died giving birth to her. He never married again, so could have no son to carry on the family name. Your father was just twenty-two, Victoria, and starting to make his way in the art world. Sir Malcolm had seen his work and been impressed, so he was invited to go and stay at Drumorchy Hall, so that Helen could sit for him. Helen was nineteen, beautiful, lively and indulged from all accounts and apparently she and John fell in love, although we only have it on hearsay, since Sir Malcolm refused to talk about the incident. Sir Malcolm was not pleased, he had hoped for better things for his daughter than a struggling sculptor, but Helen was determined and they were quickly married. What went wrong no-one will ever really know, but they weren't happy and argued a lot. Helen was pregnant and most people concluded that that was the reason for the hasty marriage. John Tremayne walked out after a particularly bad row and never

13

returned. Helen seemed to give up and became very depressed. After the birth of Ross here, she killed herself. The coroner brought in a verdict that she committed suicide whilst suffering from post-natal depression, but no-one really knew the reason and tongues wagged.'

Edward Frost stopped and looked at Vicky to see how she was taking the story, and Vicky looked at Ross. There was a bleak look in the dark-grey eyes and his mouth was clamped in a thin line.

'Oh God, how awful,' Vicky murmured, then turning to Ross, 'How is it that your name is Cameron, presumably it must have been Tremayne to start with.'

'My grandfather adopted me almost immediately after I was born and my name was registered as Cameron. He wanted nothing of John Tremayne to touch me. He hated him, still does, though he rarely mentions him.'

'He's still alive then, your grandfather?' Vicky asked.

'Oh yes. He's not too well now. He suffered a serious stroke a couple of years back and is confined to a wheelchair. He brought me up as his son and I run the estate now he's incapable of doing so.'

'I find all this hard to believe, you know,' said Vicky thoughtfully. 'It's so completely out of character. My father was always caring and loving and I just can't imagine him abandoning his wife and child.' She scrutinised Ross thoroughly and said, 'You don't look like him, you know. His colouring was like mine; you're so dark and you're much taller than he was.'

'I wouldn't know, never having seen him.' The hard look was back in Ross's eyes. 'But I'm considered to have some features similar to my grandfather.'

'Ross, you must have been absolutely furious when you learned my father had lumbered you with me, feeling as you do about him.'

'How do you know how I feel about him?' asked Ross swiftly.

'I can tell by the way your face closes up every time his name is mentioned. You don't have to concern yourself with me, you know. I shall be eighteen in two months' time—legally of age, even if my father thinks twenty-one is the age of maturity.'

'I'm sorry, I didn't mean to let my dislike of my father influence my attitude to you and you're quite wrong, you know. I admit I was stunned when I learned that my father had suddenly decided to acknowledge my existence after nearly thirty years and had made me your guardian, but now that I've met you I don't mind at all. I always thought it would be nice to have a sister or brother,' Ross said, his smile coming into play again.

At this juncture Edward Frost joined the conversation again. 'Victoria, I feel I must warn you, the terms of your father's will are binding. You cannot just ignore his wishes in regard to your guardian.'

'But he says he has left everything to me, so why can't I just manage my own affairs once I'm eighteen,' queried Vicky, a little heatedly.

'My dear, it's not as simple as that. A lot of work needs to be done to tidy up your father's financial affairs in order to assess just how much money there will be for you.' Edward Frost's brown eyes were troubled behind the thick lenses of his spectacles.

'I don't understand. Are you trying to say there won't be any money for me?' an alarmed Vicky asked.

'No, no, but your father did tend to live on his next commission,' said Edward placatingly.

'But he was highly paid. He was acknowledged as one of the best living sculptors.' Vicky realised too late what she had said and winced.

'Quite, but unfortunately he was not prolific. He was a perfectionist and spent a long time over every creation. How many did he complete in a year?' Edward asked quizzically, and added, 'Not the best method of earning a living.'

Vicky thought back and realised the solicitor was right. Her father would spend months creating a sculpture, only to scrap it and start again. He kept clients waiting, too, he always had a backlog of work. There were

16

probably a number of commissions outstanding now. She would have to do something about letting the clients know that he wouldn't be completing them now, she fretted. Her mother had always taken care of the paper work and the clients, smoothing them down when they grew impatient.

'What about life insurance? He had some, didn't he, and the insurance on the boat?'

'Yes, I believe there is some life insurance, but I suspect he was under-insured and the assessors have still to examine the wreckage of the boat to discover what caused the accident and whether they are liable to pay out,' Edward explained patiently.

Vicky said in a thin, unnaturally high voice that wobbled precariously, 'What do you mean, they have to discover the cause of the accident? I'll tell you what caused the accident. It was a freak storm and we hit a bloody great rock. I know, I was there.' Her voice had a distinct note of hysteria in it by the time she reached the end of her sentence.

'My dear child, please don't distress yourself. We will sort things out for you. There is definitely an insurance policy that John took out to cover your college fees. You've been accepted for art college, haven't you? But I do think Ross's plan is best, that you go back with him to his home in Scotland.'

'Scotland!' Vicky almost screamed the word. 'But that's the other end of the country. I've always lived in Cornwall. And what about the house, that's mine isn't it? And my A-levels? I have to take my A-levels in June or I can't even go to art college.' Vicky was definitely verging on the hysterical by now.

Ross covered her shaking fingers with his strong hand and said soothingly, 'Vicky love, calm down. You're getting yourself into such a state. We can talk about this rationally, but you must realise you can't manage here all on your own. I don't think you could cope, especially after what you've just been through. Come with me for a visit to Scotland. You're on holiday from school for Easter from next week in any case, aren't you? And you could take your A-levels up there if you stayed. There's an excellent school in Perth you could attend.' His voice was kind, but firm. Vicky got the impression that he was used to getting his own way.

She tried a further protest, but less forcefully. 'But the syllabus would probably be different in Scotland and I've already done a lot of my art folio work.'

Ross smiled, showing strong white teeth. 'Vicky, stop worrying and putting obstacles in the way. I'm certain we can arrange for you to carry on with your syllabus and for your work to be sent to the examining board you've been working for.'

There didn't seem to be anything else to say, and the minor struggle had exhausted her.

18

They were probably right, thought Vicky resignedly, she wasn't in a fit state to make decisions and arrange things for herself. She just wanted to be told what to do, in order to get, through one day at a time.

There was a knock at the door which precluded further discussion and Mrs Mead's head appeared round the door. 'Excuse me, Miss Vicky, but I've done the washing-up and tidied everywhere for you. I wondered whether you wanted me to stay with you again tonight or whether it would be all right for me to go home.'

The two men looked questioningly at Vicky and she explained, 'Mrs Mead has very kindly been sleeping here since the accident happened, so that I shouldn't be on my own.' Then she turned to Mrs Mead. 'I shall be all right now. You've been very kind, but it isn't fair to your husband and family to keep you here any longer. Thanks for all your help.'

'Well if you're sure, Miss Vicky, but I don't really like leaving you here alone,' Mrs Mead demurred.

Ross appeared to be thinking and then said, 'I shall stay here if that's all right with Vicky. I'd got to find overnight accommodation and this seems to kill two birds with one stone.'

Seeing Mrs Mead's dubious expression, he grinned and said, 'It's all right, I'm her brother.'

Mrs Mead's mouth dropped open and she

said weakly, 'Well I never. I don't know what to say.'

Vicky smiled at the thought of Mrs Mead being speechless—probably for the first time in her life—and then she thought wryly, this bit of news will be all round the village by the morning.

'Well in that case, I'll say goodnight to you, Miss Vicky, and the two gentlemen.'

'Goodnight, Mrs Mead, and thank you again for all your help,' Vicky said.

Before Mrs Mead could disappear through the door, Ross said, 'Mrs Mead, do you think you could come in tomorrow morning and give Miss Vicky a hand with her packing, she's going back to Scotland with me.'

Mrs Mead looked somewhat taken aback at this news, but said quickly, 'Of course, sir, I shall be only too pleased to help Miss Vicky any way I can.'

After she had gone Vicky turned to Ross and said mockingly, 'You have taken over, haven't you, brother Ross?'

'I'm sorry if you didn't want people to know about me, but I thought it better to let them know that everything was proper and not have the village speculating as to why you had disappeared with a strange man.'

Edward Frost stood up and stretched. 'Well if you'll excuse me I'll be getting along home. Victoria, I'll be in touch and if you have any problems don't hesitate to contact me, although I expect Ross will sort things out for you. If you leave me a note of which firms are likely to be presenting accounts to be paid for the funeral expenses, or any other outstanding bills, I'll see that they're settled without you being troubled.'

Vicky offered him her hand. 'Thank you for all your help, Mr Frost.'

'My pleasure, my dear. I hope your future is happy and trouble free.' Then he turned to Ross and said with mock severity, 'Look after her well, young man.'

'I will, sir,' was Ross's firm reply. After Edward Frost had departed, Ross said to Vicky, 'Come on, young lady, something to eat for you and then bed, I think. You look exhausted.'

'Oh Ross, I don't know whether I feel like eating,' Vicky protested.

'Whether you feel like it or not, you're getting something. I noticed you after the funeral, you had nothing at all to eat. You're too thin as it is. Come on, lead me to the kitchen and I'll make us an omelette. I have a penchant for omelettes, though I do say it myself.'

Vicky wrinkled her nose: he didn't mince words, did he? She knew she was skinny and small, she always had been.

She led him to the kitchen and showed him where the utensils and ingredients were. Very soon the smell of cooking omelettes filled the kitchen and Vicky found to her surprise that she was hungry after all. They sat one at either end of the scrubbed pine table and demolished every scrap of the fluffy omelettes he'd prepared.

'Coffee?' he asked. Vicky shook her head. 'No thanks, I don't think I'll have coffee, I'll have drinking-chocolate instead. Coffee keeps me awake and I have enough trouble sleeping as it is.'

Ross looked at her keenly. 'Have you seen your doctor since the accident?'

'Yes, of course. They took me to hospital for a check-up afterwards to make sure I hadn't been injured, but I was all right. My own doctor gave me some sleeping-pills, but I'm not too keen on taking them.'

'I should take a couple tonight, you've had a hell of a day,' Ross said sympathetically.

Vicky showed him to the guest-room and he said he'd slip out to his car and collect his overnight bag. Vicky looked surprised and said, 'Did you drive all the way? It's a long journey.'

'I took two days, I stopped overnight in the Midlands. I thought of flying, but I wasn't sure how long I'd have to stay down here or what would have to be done. I thought a car might be useful. Then again I wasn't sure how much luggage you'd have to take back with us,' Ross explained easily.

Vicky looked even more surprised. 'You

mean you had always intended for me to go back with you, even before you met me—'

'Well I didn't see how I could carry out my role of guardian from the other end of the country.'

Vicky undressed, then looked at the bottle of sleeping-tablets on the dressing-table. Should she take some? The nights she had tried sleeping without them had been beset with horrible nightmares of the accident and she'd awoken screaming in terror in a cold sweat. She didn't think she cared to risk such a occurrence with Ross Cameron sleeping in a nearby bedroom.

She tipped two tablets out and swallowed them quickly, then climbed into bed. Her last thoughts as she slipped into sleep were of Ross. Her pulse gave a jerk and she wondered why he affected her like that. 'He shouldn't do,' she told herself, 'after all he's my half-brother. But he doesn't seem like a brother. Perhaps he will when I get to know him better.'

CHAPTER TWO

The sleeping-tablets did their job well and the sun was already poking questing fingers through her curtains when Vicky woke next morning. The only problem was that the after-effects left her body feeling zombie-like and her brain like a soaked sponge. She opened her eyes and then closed them again quickly, recalling the events of the previous day. She was supposed to be packing today. She had better find out when Ross intended to depart for Scotland.

She showered and dressed in jeans and checked shirt, tied her hair up in a pony-tail and went down to the kitchen.

Ross was already up. The kitchen table was set with cereals and a carton of fresh orange juice and bowls and mugs. Ross was standing at the stove turning bacon over in a frying-pan. Vicky said dryly, 'Good-morning. What a handy man you are.'

Ross turned, grinned, ran an assessing eye over her, waved his fork and said, 'Hi, you look much better. How d'you feel?'

'Fine, apart from feeling woolly-headed from the sleeping-tablets.'

'Sit down, you'll feel even better after you've eaten. Breakfast's ready,' he said, with no trace of embarrassment at having taken over her kitchen.

'I only usually have toast,' protested Vicky, deciding to ignore the fact that he was taking her over again.

'You need a decent breakfast, we have a lot of jobs to do, and besides, like I told you, you're too thin.'

Vicky felt her irritation mounting at his high-handedness and said sharply, 'You seem

24

obsessed with my weight.'

'Nonsense, I'm just taking a brotherly interest in you,' he replied with his engaging grin, quite unperturbed by her tone.

Vicky ceased protesting and tucked into bacon and scrambled eggs and toast and marmalade, which seemed to satisfy him.

When they'd finished their coffee, she said, 'That was good, thanks, Ross,' and then followed quickly with, 'When do you want to return to Scotland?'

'Tomorrow, if we can manage it.'

Vicky felt her jaw drop and it was a few moments before she managed to gasp, 'Tomorrow! Good grief, Ross, what do you expect of me? I can't sort out and pack the accumulation of twenty years—that's how long my parents have lived here—just like that.'

'I'm not expecting you to. You don't have to do it all at once. Just take what you'll need for a holiday in Scotland—bearing in mind it's colder there than it is down here. We can always return for anything else you need when you're settled, or Mrs Mead can send it on.' Ross sounded as if there was no problem that couldn't be easily dealt with.

'What about the house? What am I supposed to do about that?'

'Mrs Mead can continue to come in and clean and keep an eye on the place, then when the solicitor has sorted out the legal details of ownership, you can decide what you want to do with it. You might like to let it out as a summer residence—that way you'd get some income from it,' Ross replied easily.

Vicky felt that she should at least make a token protest and said, 'Ross, you do realise you've just taken over and told me I'm going with you, but I don't even know where. I know nothing about you or where I'm supposed to be going to live. Don't you think you should at least tell me a few details.'

'Yes, of course, Vicky. I'm sorry, I have rather bulldozed you, haven't I? It's just that I wanted to sort everything out for you and I can't be away from the estate for too long, grandfather can't cope on his own.' Ross smiled ruefully, ran his fingers through his thick dark hair, leaving it looking in boyish disarray, and started his explanation.

'Drumorchy Hall and its estate lie between Perth and Pitlochry. For years my grandfather struggled to keep the estate going with money he made from investments. I read law at university and intended to become a barrister, but it became increasingly apparent that grandfather was going to need my help, so I went back to Drumorchy and took over the running of the estate. I persuaded my grandfather that it ought to be self-sufficient, so first we opened the gardens to the public and provided the usual amenities—a restaurant, garden shop and gift shop, and later we opened part of the house. It was

26

always too big for us, we rattled round it like two peas, so now we have one wing where we live and the public aren't allowed, and the rest of it is opened from March to October to visitors.'

'And you run the place?' Vicky chipped in thoughtfully, realising what a lot there was still to be learned about this half-brother of hers, who took his duties and obligations so seriously.

'With some help, of course. I think you'll like Drumorchy, it's very beautiful. It will make a good subject for your painting. Have you ever been to Scotland?'

'No, never. We never went very far north. We went abroad quite often and we frequently sailed across to France or the Channel Islands.' Vicky wondered why her father had never mentioned that he had lived in Scotland, but then remembered the circumstances of his stay there and realised he probably wouldn't want to remember his short time there. She thought again of what could have caused her kindly father to leave his pregnant wife and determined that she was going to find out the circumstances of that strange marriage. She knew it was useless trying to elicit information from Ross, he would just clam up—he had a blind spot where his parents were concerned— but she couldn't believe her father had just callously abandoned his wife; there must have been a reason and she intended to discover what it was, during her stay at Drumorchy Hall. Someone there would surely know something of the circumstances that had caused her father to leave.

Mrs Mead arrived at this juncture, so their conversation was abandoned. 'What do you want me to do, Miss Vicky?' she asked after eyeing Ross and greeting them both.

'If you'll wash-up and tidy the kitchen first, I'll go and start sorting out what clothing I want to take to Scotland and then perhaps you could come and help me pack,' Vicky said.

'Is there anything I can do to help you?' asked Ross.

'I don't think so, not at the moment, you wouldn't know where anything is,' replied Vicky. 'Just entertain yourself.'

'Would it be all right if I went and looked in his studio. I'd like to see his work.' Ross sounded uncertain. Strangely so for someone usually so self-assured, Vicky thought.

'Yes, of course. I'll give you the key. It's the brick building in the garden and we always keep it locked.' She got the feeling Ross wanted to be alone, almost as if he was meeting his father in some way, for the first time, so she didn't offer to go with him.

She had noticed that he hadn't said his name, or 'your' father or 'my' father when he referred to John Tremayne.

By the time she and Mrs Mead had packed the clothing she thought she might need, her school text-books and her painting materials, and she'd fended the curious questions that Mrs Mead had eagerly fired at her about this mysterious brother whom no-one knew about, Vicky decided they'd earned a break. She had a few personal possessions that she wanted to take, but she would pack them herself later. She went down to the kitchen, leaving Mrs Mead to fasten the last suitcase, and glanced around, expecting to see Ross, but the house was quiet and there was no sign of him. She switched the percolator on and then went out into the garden to look for him. She could see that the studio door was open, so she presumed he was still inside. When she peeped through the open door she could see him sitting on a stool that her father had sometimes sat on to work at his bench, his eyes fixed on a finished piece of sculpture.

She walked in softly and stood beside him and for a few moments he was completely unaware of her presence, then he looked up and said softly, with a hint of sadness in his voice, 'He was very talented, wasn't he?'

'Yes, very,' said Vicky in a choked little voice and the ever-present tears clouded her eyes again. She swallowed, not wanting to give in to her tears again, and Ross reached out for her hand and squeezed it gently, as if he understood.

He pointed with his free hand at the figure he'd been staring at and said, 'It's you, isn't it?'

Vicky remembered the photograph that had inspired her father to start the sculpture. She'd been working on the boat, wearing faded jeans and a sloppy T-shirt, her hair in a pony-tail, much as she looked now. He'd been standing on the quay and had shouted some remark about her 'swabbing the decks' and she'd turned and laughed at him, her arm outflung. He'd 'snapped' her with the camera he was carrying and later decided to sculpt her in that pose. He'd caught her mood of sheer joy and transferred it into stone; the line of her arm and the tilt of her head, even the flow of her hair, were perfectly reproduced.

She nodded at Ross, her eyes full of pain, and said huskily, 'Yes, he was doing it as a surprise for my mother's birthday. She never saw it, he always kept it covered up. He finished it the day before they died. He showed it to me, but he was going to keep it a secret and give it to her on her birthday. It would have been next week,' Vicky finished bleakly.

'What are you going to do with it? Shall you keep it yourself?' Ross asked, almost eagerly.

'I don't know. I haven't thought about it. I'm not sure I could live with it knowing why he'd done it.'

'Do you think I could have it?' Ross's voice was hesitant, as if afraid of her answer.

Vicky looked surprised. 'I suppose so. Why do you want it?'

'Because it's beautiful and because it's you and because I'd like to own something of his creating.' Ross's voice was low and intent and his grey eyes had darkened with emotion.

Vicky felt a flush stain her cheeks at his words. 'Yes, I'm sure it will be all right for you to have it. It's a personal piece, so I don't suppose it will be of interest to anyone buying his other work. I suppose some of it will have to be sold.'

'There's an awful lot of unfinished stuff, isn't there?' said Ross, glancing round the long building, with its clutter of stone blocks, wire, clay and scattered tools.

'Yes, like I told you last night, he was a bit of a perfectionist. He'd start something, it wouldn't quite come up to his expectations and he'd discard it unfinished. There are probably unfinished commissions here, too. I'll have to do some sorting out and let people know that their work won't be finished.'

'Leave it for now, they'll probably realise what's happened, in any case. His death was written about in all the newspapers,' Ross said firmly.

Vicky continued to pursue her own line of thought. 'The trouble was, he'd down tools at the drop of a hat. He'd suddenly say, "Come on, I'm having a day off" or "a week off," and he'd whisk my mother and quite often me, too, away on some expedition. I suppose it wasn't conducive to completing a piece of work.'

31

'No, I shouldn't imagine it would be,' agreed Ross rather dryly.

'Have you seen all you want to see? I came to ask you if you wanted coffee.'

'Yes, can I take my sculpture with me now?' asked Ross, his eyes wandering back to it again.

'You might as well. It will be one less thing to dispose of when the time comes to clear this place,' said Vicky with a slight quaver in her voice. Finding the piece of white fabric that had covered the statuette and wrapping it up firmly, she picked it up and dumped it into Ross's arms. 'Come on, coffee and then back to work.' She followed Ross out and turned to lock the door.

Somehow she managed to finish her sorting and packing, leaving only the things she would need to use in the morning to be packed, and they put everything ready in the hall to be put in Ross's car.

Vicky eyed it dubiously. 'It looks an awful lot; will it all go in?'

'I should think so, it's quite a big car and we can put things on the back seat as there's only the two of us to fit in,' Ross said.

Vicky nodded. She'd seen the car. It was a silver Mercedes. She'd thought 'expensive,' but hadn't commented.

'Do you drive?' Ross asked.

'Yes, but I've only just passed my test and I've only driven on the roads round here. I need practice on motorways and in busy towns,' Vicky said, alarmed in case he thought she would be able to do some driving on the way to Scotland.

As if reading her thoughts, Ross laughed. 'Don't worry, we'll find you something smaller and less powerful than my car for you to practise with, but it will be useful for you to be able to drive yourself around when you're in Scotland.'

They set off the following morning as planned. Mrs Mead hugged Vicky, mopped up a few tears and said fiercely to Ross, 'Mind you take good care of her.'

'I will,' promised Ross and added. 'She'll be coming back to see you, never fear.'

Ross pressed on, with short breaks, until they got into Cheshire and then announced that this was as far as they were going. 'There's a pleasant hotel I've stayed at once or twice. We'll book in there.'

Vicky had dozed, chatted, listened to taped music and dozed again on the journey. The big car was comfortable and roomy and she didn't feel particularly tired, but she realised Ross must be getting weary of driving, the M5 and M6 had been busy.

They pulled up in front of an attractive hotel in a pleasant country setting and Ross extricated their overnight cases from the back seat of the car. 'We'll leave everything else, there's no point in unpacking all that luggage only to have to repack it in the morning.'

They were shown to what was really a small suite of rooms. Vicky was shown into her bedroom from which a door led into a small sitting-room. Ross's bedroom led off the other side of the sitting-room and each bedroom had its own tiny bathroom.

Ross said, 'I'm going to shower. We can either have dinner in the dining-room or in our own sitting-room. I'll leave it to you to decide.'

Vicky took a leisurely bath and was glad she'd packed a dress in her overnight bag. She'd been wearing rust-coloured cords and a dark-brown sweater to travel in, but the hotel was high-class and she would have felt uncomfortable going down to dinner so casually dressed. She slipped into the grey silk jersey dress and high-heeled black shoes and brushed her hair, leaving it loose, and made up her face carefully. Then she went to find Ross. He was stretched out in an armchair in the sitting-room, watching television, but he glanced round when he heard the door open. He raised his eyebrows, whistled softly and said teasingly, 'Very nice. I shall be the envy of all the males in the dining-room. I presume we are dining in public.'

Vicky felt the usual tell-tale blush staining her cheeks and wished fervently that she could be blasé about his teasing and think of witty replies. She decided their acquaintance was of too short a duration and hoped that when she

34

got used to being with him she could treat him in a more sisterly manner.

'If you want to. I don't really mind where we eat. If you want to stay here, that's fine by me,' Vicky assured him.

'No, we'll dine downstairs. It would be a pity if only I saw you, now you've gone to so much trouble,' Ross said seriously, but with a teasing gleam in his eye.

'I haven't gone to so much trouble,' protested Vicky indignantly. 'You'd think I usually looked a mess.'

'I'm sorry, I didn't mean to infer that, I only meant you looked very attractive,' Ross soothed. He held out his arm to her, 'Come on, let's eat.'

Vicky discovered she was hungry and was inordinately pleased about it, her appetite had been poor since the accident. She tucked into soup, followed by halibut in a delicious sauce, and finished off with a large slice of chocolate and cream gateau. Ross had cheese and biscuits, but nodded approvingly and grinned at her as she plunged her spoon into the gooey confectionery.

They took their coffee in a small adjoining lounge and Vicky, as if suddenly remembering, said hesitantly, 'Ross, does your grandfather know you're bringing me back with you? How will he feel about me, feeling as he does about my father?'

'Yes, he knows. I told him about my being

appointed as your guardian before I went to the funeral. I don't think he'll let his feelings towards your father influence his manner towards you. He's always been marvellous to me, he's all the family I've ever had, and, after all, you and I do share the same father,' Ross said placatingly.

'That's different. He loves you because you're his daughter's child,' Vicky protested, her brow wrinkled.

Ross leaned towards her and ran firm but gentle fingers over the furrows. 'Stop spoiling your pretty forehead with worrying about something that's not going to happen.'

Ross wanted to get off straight after breakfast the following morning, so he advised her to have an early night. He escorted her to her bedroom door, dropped a quick, light kiss on her forehead and said, 'Sleep well, Vicky.'

Vicky wandered into her room thinking, 'I hope I do, but perhaps I'd better make sure and take two sleeping-tablets.' Then she remembered. She hadn't brought them. They had been sitting on her dressing-table when she'd taken them the previous evening and she had intended putting them in her handbag this morning, but had forgotten.

She undressed and climbed into bed, hoping fervently that her recurring nightmare would leave her in peace. She lay awake for some time, half afraid to close her eyes, but tiredness eventually overtook her.

It was happening again. The sea, the hungry sea was clawing at her, trying to consume her. She could see her parents drowning, but could not get to them to help. She struggled frantically, heard a thin unearthly scream and didn't realise that it came from her own throat.

Strong arms were holding her. She was safe. She clung to the solid, reassuring body against which she was pressed, burying her face against the warm, clean-smelling skin. A voice was saying reassuringly, 'It's all right, little one, you're quite safe. Nothing is going to harm you,' and a hand was gently stroking her hair.

Vicky opened her eyes and eased herself away from the warm comfort of Ross's chest. She noticed that he was wearing a short towelling robe over a pair of pyjama bottoms. The robe was held together by a belt, but the top was open revealing a broad chest with a fine covering of dark hair. Colour flooded her face as she realised it had been his chest she had burrowed into and that she was clad only in a thin cotton nightdress and that Ross's arms were tight around her.

'I'm sorry I've disturbed you. I must have had a nightmare. Did I make a lot of noise?' she asked anxiously, hoping she hadn't disturbed everyone in the hotel.

'Well, your screams were a bit unearthly. It must have been one helluva nightmare you were having,' he said, eyeing her questioningly.

She nodded, remembering again the

37

vividness of her dream.

'It's the accident, isn't it?' he asked gently.

'Yes. I keep dreaming about it, unless I take sleeping-tablets, and I've forgotten to bring them with me.'

'Look, I'll get you a drink. It will calm you and help you to get back to sleep again.' Ross headed towards the sitting-room.

He returned, carrying a glass of amber liquid. Vicky eyed it suspiciously. 'What is it?'

'Only brandy, with a drop of hot water and sugar in. It will settle your nerves. I would have got you some hot milk if I could, but all we've got are those silly little one-cup-of-tea containers of milk.'

Vicky sipped the brandy and found that Ross was right. The shaking in her limbs had stopped and she felt calmer. She still felt reluctant to go back to sleep, afraid that the terrifying dream would return.

As if reading her thoughts, Ross said gently, 'Vicky, have you talked about this to anyone? Seen a doctor?'

'I saw my doctor after the accident, it was he who prescribed the sleeping-tablets,' Vicky said shortly.

Ross persisted. 'Have you really talked through what happened when the boat capsized? Sometimes talking about bad experiences can help the mind to come to terms with them.'

'You mean the old psychoanalysis

approach.' Vicky sounded sceptical. 'I haven't gone into great detail, but I had to make a statement to the police about what happened.'

'Tell me. Not just the facts, but how you felt at the time. I think it might help.' Ross covered her hands, which were nervously picking at the bedcover, and forced her to return his gaze, his grey eyes holding hers like a magnet.

Vicky looked at him for a few moments, as if trying to come to a decision, then swallowed and plunged into her story, her voice little more than a husky whisper.

'It was a perfect day for sailing, blustery breeze, but nothing we hadn't coped with many times before. Sunny, with bits of cloud, but nothing that looked particularly ominous. We weren't so very far from the shore either. We'd been tacking up and down off the coastline. Then this squall blew up. I've never experienced anything like it. They said afterwards that it was a freak storm. One moment we were sailing along quite happily, the next a gale-force wind was blowing, lightning was flashing, and torrential rain was soaking us. Before we could get the canvas down, the mast had snapped. We got the sails down as best we could and Dad tried to start the engine, but it wouldn't start. We were shipping a lot of water and were completely off course. There's a ridge of rocks and we must have sailed too near to them. The next minute we'd hit a rock and the boat just rose up in the air and overturned. We were all wearing life jackets, but Mum and Dad were trapped under the boat. I was thrown clear and managed to grab a piece of wood that had splintered off the hull. I was frantic. I tried to get to my parents to help them, but it was hopeless. The seas were so high. I could feel the current pulling at me. I was sure I was going to drown. Then the lifeboat arrived. Another boat had seen what had happened to us and alerted them. They searched for my parents, but there was no trace. They were both washed up on shore the following day.' Vicky finished, suddenly aware that her cheeks were wet with tears.

Ross had his arm around her and produced a large white handkerchief from the pocket of his robe and wiped her face.

While she had been talking she had been reliving the horror of the incident, but now she felt better. Drained, as if a catharsis had taken place, and weary, so weary. Her limbs felt heavy and her eyelids wouldn't stay open. She said tiredly, 'I think I shall sleep now,' and lay back against the pillows.

Ross covered her, tucking her in as if she were a child. She murmured sleepily, 'Thank you, Ross, for being here.' He bent and dropped the softest of kisses on her lips.

In the brief moment before sleep completely encompassed her, she recalled the satisfying feel of Ross's arms around her and the gentle kiss he had given her and felt a strange, hitherto unknown warmth deep within her. A niggling voice told her she really shouldn't be feeling this way about her brother, but she was too tired to think it through and told herself she'd sort it all out in the morning.

CHAPTER THREE

The following morning when Vicky opened the curtains, it was to find the sunshine gone and a grey, overcast sky outside. As they got further north the rain started and by the time they were driving over Shap Fell, the rain was torrential and the lowering sky so dark that Ross was driving with his headlights on and the windscreen wipers were working overtime. Speed restrictions had been imposed on the motorway and the traffic had built up until they were crawling nose to tail in all three lanes.

'I think we might as well stop at the next service-station and have coffee and hopefully this downpour will ease,' said Ross ruefully. 'There's no joy driving through this.'

By the time they'd finished their coffee and were on the road again the rain had eased and the traffic was moving at a more reasonable speed. They made fairly good time until they got on the A74 in the Border country and then they suddenly ground to a complete halt. They sat in an unmoving line of vehicles, not knowing what was wrong, and then a police car, followed closely by an ambulance, flashed by with their klaxons blaring and lights flashing.

'An accident, do you think?' asked Vicky anxiously.

'Looks that way,' agreed Ross and added, 'We could be here for hours whilst they get the road cleared and the traffic moving again. If I'd had a bit more notice I could have got off onto a minor road and taken a roundabout route. As it is we're stuck now and we don't even know how far ahead the start of the hold-up is.'

Ross fished out a packet of biscuits and a flask of tea and they sat eating, drinking and chatting until eventually the traffic started to move slowly again. The accident had occurred about ten miles ahead. They eventually passed the mangled wreckage of two cars that originally had been blocking both lanes, but had now been moved to the side of the road.

Ross had planned to be home by late afternoon, but the hold-ups had delayed them and it was early evening before they eventually drove through a pair of large wrought-iron gates and up a long, gravelled drive. The light was fading earlier than usual because of the greyness of the day. A steady drizzle was falling and mist hung about the large house. Vicky peered through the windscreen, trying to make out what the house looked like. It looked huge and grey and menacing and a shiver ran down her spine. She wondered what awaited her here. It wasn't a very welcoming sight, she thought nervously.

As if reading her mind, Ross said cheerfully, 'Sorry it's such a dismal start for your first impressions of your new home. It isn't always like this, though I must admit we do get a fair bit of rain.'

He ushered her up the wide sweep of steps that led to the huge studded front door and swung the door open, saying, 'I'll get Thompson to get the luggage out for us.'

Vicky felt a little better as she glanced round the large, square entrance hall. A crystal chandelier bathed the room in light; stags' heads and portraits, presumably of Ross's ancestors, lined the oak-panelled walls. The floor was tiled in Italian marble, but a large, square Persian carpet in deep-reds and blues covered the centre portion. The room, however, was dominated by a magnificent stone fireplace, in which a log fire blazed. Vicky felt herself drawn towards it and stretched out her hands to the cheerful glow.

'Are you cold? Would you like a sherry before you see your room?' Ross asked, casting her an anxious glance.

'No, I'm not really cold. It's just that the fire

looked so welcoming after the damp greyness outside, but a sherry would be nice,' Vicky assured him.

'I'm sorry it's been such a dismal journey for you,' he said apologetically. 'I did warn you it would be colder up here than in Cornwall.'

Vicky glanced at his face, detecting the lines of weariness there, realising that he'd done a lot of travelling over the past few days and that the journey that day had been particularly trying.

'I'm fine, but you must be worn out after all the driving you've done,' she said sympathetically.

He led the way through a door at the right of the hall, into a carpeted passageway, saying over his shoulder, 'This is our private wing of the house. I'll show you round the visitors' part tomorrow.'

He opened a door into what appeared to be a small sitting-room, carpeted in rusts and fawns, with settees and armchairs in velvet in a darker shade of rust. 'Make yourself comfortable,' he said, as he walked over to where a drinks cabinet stood. He came over to where she sat and handed her a small glass of sherry, then he stood with an arm on the marble mantelpiece and looked down at her.

'I'll get Mrs Thompson to show you your room and you can have a rest and get yourself sorted out before dinner.'

Her room was spacious and beautiful, with a

huge bed, deep rose-pink drapes, and tall windows curtained in the same shade. The curtains were drawn and the effect, combined with the light shed from rose-shaded lamps, was to cast a warm, rosy glow over the room, making it look welcoming.

Mrs Thompson said gently, 'I hope you'll be comfortable and happy here. Poor wee bairn, you've had a dreadful time, haven't you?'

Vicky's eyes filled with tears at the concern in her voice and she said huskily, 'I'm sure I shall. My room is perfectly beautiful.'

Mrs Thompson looked hard at her face for a moment and then said, 'You look like your father.'

'You knew him?' asked Vicky, eagerly surprised that she had so soon found someone who remembered him.

Mrs Thompson hesitated, as if trying to make up her mind about something and then said, 'Yes I knew him. Of course it was a long time ago, over thirty years, and I was only a young parlour-maid then.' Then she added, almost defiantly, 'I liked him. And I never believed all the things that were said about him.' She changed the subject abruptly, as if afraid that she'd said too much. 'Do you want me to help you unpack, Miss Victoria?'

Vicky could have hugged her. It was so good to find someone here, on Ross's territory, who didn't condemn her father out of hand, but she realised it was too soon and she would have to tread warily if she was to get the full story out of Mrs Thompson. 'No, I can manage, thank you. I haven't brought so very much luggage.'

She had noted that her cases were arranged neatly side by side. Thompson must have brought them up whilst she was having her sherry.

'Well, if you're sure, I'll go and see about dinner. I expect you and Master Ross will be ready for it.' And she bustled out.

Vicky unpacked and stowed her clothing in the huge polished oak hanging-cupboards. They didn't take up much space, the cupboards were so roomy. She showered and decided she would wear the grey dress again. She didn't possess many dresses. They hadn't entertained a great deal in Cornwall. She'd practically lived in jeans, but she thought something better would be expected of her here. She would have to buy herself some more clothes if she were staying here permanently. She was surprised to find that her mind had now readily accepted the possibility that had so shocked her three days before, that she should remain in Scotland with Ross.

She wondered where they would be eating. She realised she only knew where the little sitting-room was. She need not have worried for, as she was making her way down the staircase, Ross was walking across the hallway.

'Hello there. Is your room to your liking?'

46

he asked, smiling up at her.

'It's quite beautiful. Thank you for putting me somewhere so pleasant,' Vicky said, slightly breathlessly. Ross had changed into black slacks and a white sweater and looked very handsome.

'My pleasure. It's got rather a nice balcony, with a view over the estate. I thought you might find it a good place to paint, though there is a room at the top of the house with a large window that you might like to use as a studio. You can look it over tomorrow.'

Vicky stretched out her hand and laid it on his arm and squeezed, to show him how thrilled she was. He patted her hand, rather in the manner of an indulgent uncle, and said, 'We'll eat in the snug, it's cosier than the dining-room. Grandfather is dining in his room tonight. He hasn't been too well today.'

Vicky glanced at his face, trying to assess whether he was telling the whole truth and said hesitantly, 'Ross, is it because I'm here that your grandfather is dining in his room tonight?'

'No, not really. He has had a bad day. He gets good days and bad days. But he's reticent about eating with strangers, because he's paralysed down one side. He has to have his food cut up for him and sometimes he drops bits of food when he's trying to get it into his mouth. He's very proud and doesn't like people seeing him like that. He'll be fine when he's got to know you,' Ross reassured her.

Vicky discovered that the little sitting-room was called 'the snug' and a circular table had been laid for two in there. She and Ross dined on Scotch broth, salmon, and raspberry tart and cream.

'That was delicious. Does Mrs Thompson do the cooking?' asked Vicky, wondering how many staff there were.

'Yes; she has some help, of course, but we don't have so many staff, now. We had a bevy of folk working here when I was a boy, but in the interests of economy we've had to cut down. Although we've taken on extra staff since we've opened the house to the public. If we carry out an idea we've been kicking around, to have banquets and receptions here, we shall have to take on more catering staff. Grandfather's not too keen on the idea. I think he's always relieved when the public vacate the place at five o'clock and doesn't relish having them here in the evening, but it's proved a real money-spinner in other "stately homes", so I suppose we shouldn't reject the idea without consideration,' Ross stated philosophically.

'Shall you mind?' asked Vicky, curious as to how he felt about having his home invaded by the paying public.

'I suppose I'd rather not have to resort to these measures, but it was either that or vacating the place and handing it over to the National Trust. We couldn't have gone on as we were. It was just a millstone round our necks. Now at least it's paying its own way. I think I'd rather have it on those conditions than lose it altogether. I'm rather fond of the old place,' he finished, striving for a lighter tone.

'Ross, I'd like to help whilst I'm here, if there's something I can do,' Vicky offered shyly.

He looked surprised. 'I didn't bring you here to work. I brought you for a holiday. Besides you won't have a lot of spare time. Presumably you have to work for your A-levels. What subjects are you doing? I never thought to ask you. Art, obviously.'

Vicky nodded. 'Art, English Lit. and History.'

'Oh well, in that case I'll introduce you to the library tomorrow. You should find it useful. We'll sort out your school for you, too. I have one in mind, in Perth. I'll give the headmistress a ring and fix up an interview and you can go and see what you think of it.'

They chatted about books for a while and then Vicky suddenly gave a great yawn and Ross said dryly, 'Bed for you, I think, young lady. It's been a long day. I could do with an early night myself.'

Vicky stood up and waited uncertainly, wondering if he would kiss her, as he had done the previous evening, albeit a fraternal kiss. But he didn't, he merely smiled and said,

'Sleep well, Vicky. No nightmares tonight, eh?'

*   *   *

As soon as Vicky awoke next morning, she rushed to the window, eager to see her balcony and the view. She pulled the heavy drapes back impatiently, unlocked the window that opened out onto the balcony and stepped out. She gasped at the view that met her eyes. The rain had cleared and the sun shone from an April blue sky, setting a million diamond drops glistening in the green, lush lawns.

A breath-taking view of the glen, the loch and the surrounding mountains was only interrupted by the belts of Scots pine, Douglas firs and rowans that encircled the estate grounds. Ross had not exaggerated about the view.

She glanced quickly at her watch, surprised to find that it was already half-past eight. She had slept soundly, without stirring, for several hours and now felt fresh and eager to sample a new day.

She showered and dressed quickly in a yellow sweater and jeans and tied her hair back with a thin yellow ribbon. Then she headed downstairs at the gallop.

Not knowing quite where to go, she headed towards a door from which faint sounds of conversation and the chink of crockery could be heard. She opened the door and peered in,

50

to find herself surveying the kitchen, where Mrs Thompson and a young girl were working and chatting.

Mrs Thompson glanced up quickly. 'Good morning, Miss Victoria. Are you ready for your breakfast? I would have sent it up for you, but Master Ross said to let you sleep as long as you wanted to.'

'Good morning, Mrs Thompson. Is Ross up then?' Vicky asked.

'Lord bless you, yes. Hours ago. He's out riding. Where would you like to eat your breakfast? The dining-room is a bit large for one, but you could have it in the snug or the conservatory. That's very pleasant, particularly when the sun is shining.'

'I'd rather stay here in the kitchen and chat to you, whilst I'm eating, if you don't mind,' said Vicky, heading towards a long table and sitting down.

Mrs Thompson looked taken aback for a moment and then smiled. 'No, of course I don't mind. That's what Master Ross does quite often. What would you like? Cereal, orange juice, bacon and eggs?'

'Just juice and toast and coffee, please. I don't eat much breakfast,' said Vicky firmly.

Mrs Thompson looked dubious. 'Master Ross said you had to have a proper breakfast.'

'Oh piffle. He's got this crazy notion that I'm undernourished and need fattening up. There's absolutely nothing wrong with me. I just don't eat much in a morning,' Vicky said in a tone that brooked no further argument.

Mrs Thompson shook her head reproachfully. 'I don't know about you young girls. Always dieting and eating these convenience foods.' But she produced a jug of orange juice and a rack of toast without further argument.

Vicky found herself tucking into more toast than she usually ate, probably due to the delicious apricot preserve that she was liberally spreading it with. Mrs Thompson's own special recipe, she was told.

Mrs Thompson had introduced the young girl as Morag Mackenzie and then shooed her off to put some washing in the washing-machine, in what Vicky took to be a utility room which led off the kitchen.

Vicky had just persuaded Mrs Thompson to have a cup of coffee with her when the door suddenly opened and in came Ross. Vicky turned to watch him. He looked virile and handsome in riding-breeches, boots and a polo-necked sweater and tweed hacking-jacket.

He smiled when he saw her and said cheerfully, 'Good morning, Vicky. I see you've surfaced. Did you sleep well?'

'Like a top. You've been up for hours, I hear,' Vicky said, removing a crumb of toast from her chin.

'Well not so long, but I like to try and get a

ride in before I start work.' He wandered over towards the table and then leaned over her to help himself to a slice of toast. As he did so Vicky caught the scent of leather, horses and Ross's aftershave. It was a heady mixture and caused her pulse to trip a few extra beats.

He waved the slice of toast at her. 'Is this all you're having? I thought I said you had to have a proper breakfast,' he said with mock severity.

'Ross, I haven't done anything to work up an appetite,' protested Vicky mildly.

'Right, Madam. Tomorrow we'll have you up and you can come riding with me. That'll work up an appetite. You do ride, I suppose?' he asked, with a frown, as if unable to comprehend why anyone wouldn't.

A little thrill of pleasure went through Vicky at the thought of riding with him. 'Well I had a pony and rode regularly when I was a child, but I haven't done so much in latter years. Just occasionally I've hired a hack from some nearby stables and gone pony-trekking. You'll have to bear with me if I'm rusty,' Vicky said apologetically.

'We'll find you a nice quiet mount and take it steady for a few days and then you'll be fine. You don't forget how to ride,' Ross said complacently. 'Is there some coffee left in that pot,' pushing a cup towards her and then reverting to their previous discussion. 'Did you win lots of lovely little rosettes when you were riding as a child?' he teased.

'A few. Nothing very important. Just local shows. I don't think I was all that good. I probably looked like one of the little girls in those horsey cartoons. You know, big fat ponies and little girls perched on top with pigtails sticking out either side.'

Ross roared with laughter and choked on his toast. Vicky thumped his back.

Their hilarity was interrupted by a cool voice saying, 'What a homely little scene. Ross, darling, I see you are back at last. Are we going to do any work today?'

There was an uneasy silence and Vicky noticed Mrs Thompson's mouth tighten, then she started noisily loading crockery into the dish-washer.

Ross filled the silence. 'Good morning, Alison. Vicky, this is Alison MacLeod, my girl Friday. Alison, this is Vicky Tremayne.'

Vicky let her eyes wander over the girl to whom the clipped tones belonged. She was probably in her mid-twenties. Small and curvy, with a cap of short, shiny black hair, dark eyes and a full, red mouth. She looked almost gypsy-like, but there was nothing of the gypsy in her dress. She wore a slim, form-fitting black skirt and a red silk blouse. Very high heels gave her added height. She was a very attractive package and Vicky felt strangely depressed.

'So this is the mysterious little sister. How d'you do?' She managed to make the remark sound insulting somehow and the hand that she stretched out towards Vicky barely brushed her fingers. The laughter had suddenly gone from the morning. Vicky couldn't understand why, but she suddenly felt as if she had just made an enemy.

Ross said smoothly, as if the barbs had never been uttered, 'I'm not working this morning, Alison. I'm showing Vicky round the house. You can deal with any pressing matters and I'll sort out anything that is outstanding this afternoon.'

Colour tinged the girl's cheeks and her dark eyes looked stormy. 'But Ross, you've been away six days and there's a lot of things to be settled before the house opens on Good Friday.'

'We've got over a week before then; there's nothing that can't wait another day,' Ross soothed.

'Well, have you made a decision about opening for banquets and receptions? The advertisers are wanting to know,' she persisted.

'I think we'll leave that in abeyance at the moment. Grandfather isn't too keen on the idea,' Ross said, with an edge to his voice.

'Oh really, Ross. As if it matters what he thinks. The place is yours. Why don't you make your own decision?' she said bitingly.

'It matters to me what he thinks. And if you don't mind I'd rather leave this discussion until a more suitable time, in the privacy of the office.' There was definite ice in Ross's voice now.

'Well I'll get on then. Some of us have work to do.' She swung on her heels and strode out, her heels tapping agitatedly on the tiled floor.

Vicky felt like someone at a tennis match, her eyes had been shifting between the two combatants in the verbal battle. She'd almost felt like scoring for them—'Advantage MacLeod, deuce, advantage Cameron.'

The atmosphere was almost tangible after she had left and Mrs Thompson said something that sounded like 'Hmph' and slammed the dish-washer shut.

Ross shrugged and raised his eyebrows. 'She's a marvellous organiser and takes a load of work off my shoulders, but sometimes she gets a bit officious.' He looked at Vicky, as if trying to make her understand. 'I'll just go and change, I smell of horse, and then I'll be back to take you on your conducted tour.'

'Ross, if you're busy, don't worry about me. I can wander about by myself,' Vicky said miserably, feeling responsible for all the aggression in the air.

'Don't be silly. I want to take you round. I've been looking forward to it. Have another cup of coffee while you wait. I'll only be a few minutes. All right?' he asked, seeing Vicky's troubled blue eyes and touching her cheek with his forefinger.

When he had gone, Mrs Thompson said

56

shortly, 'I know it's none of my business, because she doesn't interfere with me, but if you ask me, she's far too officious. You'd think she owned the place, the way she takes over and gives her orders. I can't stand her.'

Vicky made no reply, but knowing how Mrs Thompson felt about Alison made things a little better. Then she remembered the 'darling' and wondered whether there was more between Ross and Alison MacLeod than just an employer and employee relationship. She said slowly, 'How long has she worked for Ross?'

'Two years. She came when Sir Malcolm had his stroke and was so ill. Poor Master Ross couldn't cope with his grandfather and all the administrative work on his own. She's good at her job, you've got to give her that,' Mrs Thompson admitted grudgingly. 'She copes with the office work and acts as one of the guides, taking people round the house.'

'Where does she live?' asked Vicky, fearful that she lived at the house, although she hadn't seen her the previous evening.

'In the village. She's got a house there that belonged to her parents. She lived there as a child. She and Master Ross had known each other for years, but then she went away to college and worked in London, I think it was, for a time. Then when her parents died and Master Ross advertised for an assistant, she applied and came back here to live.'

'What did she mean about Ross owning the estate? I thought it belonged to his grandfather,' asked Vicky curiously.

'Sir Malcolm made it over to Master Ross when he became ill. Something about it being easier for him to administer and less death duties when anything happens to Sir Malcolm,' explained Mrs Thompson. Then, as if remembering her place, 'I shouldn't be discussing this with you, it's not proper. You ask Master Ross if you want to know anything.'

Ross returned then and they set off on their tour of the house. Vicky found it truly fascinating as Ross talked about all the treasures they were seeing. She became sated with so much beauty that she was barely able to take it all in. Gobelin tapestries, Adam ceilings and fireplaces, Grinling Gibbons carvings, Sheraton, Chippendale and Hepplewhite furniture, Aubusson carpets; all designed to delight the eye. Vicky turned shining eyes to him. 'Ross, everywhere is so beautiful. No wonder you couldn't bear to part with it.'

When he showed her the library, lined with bookcases housing thousands of books, he smiled and said, 'There you are, you should be able to find some books of interest to you.'

'Can I really come in here and use the books?' Vicky asked incredulously.

'Of course, that's what they're there for. It's no use having books if you never use them.'

In the drawing-room were two portraits, obviously mother and daughter, although they were painted in different styles. Seeing her scrutiny Ross said, 'My mother and grandmother.' They were both very beautiful, golden-haired and blue-eyed. Vicky vaguely wondered where Ross's storm-grey eyes had come from, since both his parents had had vivid blue eyes. It was from their father that she had inherited her own deep-blue eyes. 'Perhaps his grandfather's are grey,' she thought. 'They're both very beautiful. No wonder your grandfather was so devastated,' she said sympathetically.

He took her up to the little turret room that he had said she could use as a studio. It was perfect for that purpose. It was circular and had large windows all round the walls, which gave an abundance of light.

'Ross, it will make an absolutely marvellous studio,' Vicky enthused.

'Your father used it when he stayed here,' he said abruptly.

Vicky smiled sadly, noting that he had said 'your' father. Obviously he still couldn't bring himself to own John Tremayne as his father.

She discovered that Alison was lunching with them. The knowledge rather took the sparkle from the morning. Vicky ate silently. Ross and Alison did all the talking, discussing estate business. Ross glanced at her once or twice, as if puzzled by her lack of enthusiasm, after her effervescence of the morning.

He tried to involve her in the conversation, but she felt young and gauche beside the older, sophisticated girl and could think of nothing to say. Alison tended to monopolise the conversation. Her fury of the morning obviously forgotten, she was charm personified towards Ross, now.

CHAPTER FOUR

That evening Vicky and Sir Malcolm met. She had spent the afternoon walking round the grounds. Ross and Alison had gone off to work in the office. Vicky had wandered round, admiring the daffodils that grew amongst the grass and in the borders; she noticed the faint first tinge of colour in the rhododendron buds that promised a colourful display later, and enjoyed the exotic blooms in the glasshouses. She had peeped in the windows of the café and the shop, not yet open, and drifted round to the stables, wondering which of the horses Ross would give her tomorrow.

All the estate workers she met had been polite and friendly and she had really quite enjoyed her afternoon, but she wished Ross had been free to go round with her.

She hadn't seen him at all since lunchtime and when she went downstairs for dinner she wondered where they would be eating.

She had dressed in a black velvet skirt and a white frilly blouse and had put her hair up. She decided, with satisfaction, that she looked quite sophisticated and wished she had looked like that in the morning; perhaps she could have held her own in the presence of Alison MacLeod, if she had.

She peered into the 'snug', but it was empty, so she poked her head round the kitchen door and said, 'Where are we eating tonight, Mrs Thompson?'

'Oh, in the dining-room, of course, dear. Sir Malcolm has come down tonight. Everything has to be very proper for him.'

Vicky wended her way slowly towards the large, formal, dining-room. Butterflies fluttered in her stomach at the thought of meeting Ross's grandfather. She wondered nervously how he would treat her.

She opened the door slowly and stood uncertainly in the half-open doorway. She took in the scene before her as if it were a tableau: Ross standing in front of the fireplace, a glass in his hand, looking down at the thin figure in a wheelchair.

Ross glanced up and saw her. 'Well come in, Vicky. Don't hover in the doorway.'

She walked slowly towards him, aware of the unblinking scrutiny of the old man. She heard the muttered comment, 'So this is Tremayne's brat. She looks like him,' and

61

Ross's low reproof, 'Grandfather, you promised.'

'So I did. I'm sorry. Come here, child. Let's look at you.'

She walked closer and then stopped and forced herself to meet his eyes. They were ice-blue and she remembered later feeling surprised about this, she had been sure they would be grey. His hair was thick, but completely white. His face was gaunt and there was a droop to his right eye and the right-hand corner of his mouth. 'That must be the side that's paralysed,' Vicky thought. In spite of his age and the effect of his stroke, there was a vague look of Ross about him.

'Good evening, Victoria,' he said, in the paper-thin, slightly slurred voice. 'Don't look so nervous, I'm not going to eat you.'

'Good evening, Sir Malcolm. Are you feeling better this evening?' Vicky asked, with a slight quiver in her voice.

'Better than I was, I suppose. At my age one doesn't hope for too much,' he said wryly.

Ross had gone over to a table and now returned with a drink for her. 'Sherry, Vicky?'

'Thank you.' She looked gratefully, at Ross, pleased to have something to do with her hands and with the thought that if she were drinking she couldn't be expected to converse.

Ross let his eyes roam over her and then said dryly, 'Very chic. Quite the beautiful lady, tonight, eh?'

62

Dinner was served and Vicky managed to contribute to the conversation. Ross asked her about her afternoon and they chatted about the gardens and the horses. Vicky pointedly avoided looking at Sir Malcolm as Ross cut his food up for him and tucked his large table napkin under his chin. He managed very well, she thought, using a fork in his left hand. His right hand hung limply in his lap.

He didn't stay up long after dinner. Ross took him back to his room and then she and Ross watched a film on television.

It was a couple of days later when she had an encounter with him that probably changed their relationship and made her think he wasn't the monster she had first imagined. She had gone to the library to look for a book on the Civil War that Ross had told her was there. As she was about to retrace her steps, after finding the book, she noticed that Sir Malcolm was sitting near the window. There was a book on his lap, but his eyes were closed. She was concerned in case he was ill and went over to him, saying, 'Are you feeling all right, Sir Malcolm?'

'Yes, I'm all right. I've been trying to read, but this damned right eye keeps wandering and the lid keeps drooping. I end up seeing double.'

Then, greatly daring, the words seemingly popping out before she had stopped to think about them, Vicky said, 'Would you like me to read to you?'

His pale-blue eyes swivelled to her face and she felt hot colour wash her cheeks at his scrutiny. 'Are you sure? Can you spare the time? Ross tells me you're working for A-levels.'

Vicky nodded. 'Yes, I can spare an hour or so, until coffee-time.'

He handed her the book. It was *The Mayor of Casterbridge* by Thomas Hardy. Vicky was very familiar with it. It had been a work she had studied in class. She read in her low, attractive voice. Sir Malcolm leaned back in his high-backed chair and closed his eyes. She read on. She wondered if he had gone to sleep, but when she hesitated about starting a new chapter, he opened his eyes and said, 'Tired of reading?'

'Oh no, I thought perhaps you were tired of listening.'

'Indeed no. You have a very attractive voice. It's a very pleasurable experience listening to you,' he said thoughtfully.

She continued reading until Mrs Thompson brought coffee. 'I wondered where you were. I didn't realise you were down here, Sir Malcolm. Master Ross said Miss Vicky was working in the library.'

'She's been reading to me,' he said.

'That's nice,' smiled Mrs Thompson.

They drank their coffee together in companionable silence and then Vicky said, 'I could read to you each day, at some time, if you'd like that.'

'Thank you, my dear. You're a kind girl.'

*   *   *

Vicky and Ross had established the habit of riding together before breakfast. On the first morning, she had been awoken by Ross banging on her bedroom door and coming in with a cup of tea for her. 'Come on, it's seven-thirty. I'll give you fifteen minutes to be up, dressed and downstairs ready to ride,' he said briskly.

Vicky stared at him with smoky, sleep-drenched eyes and muttered, 'Goodness, Ross. You're disgustingly energetic first thing in a morning.' But she drank her tea and dressed quickly and was actually downstairs with a couple of minutes to spare.

Ross was already there. Vicky said, 'Ross, I presume I'm all right dressed like this,' pointing to her cord pants and chunky sweater, 'but I've no hat or boots, you know.'

'I can find you some, there are some spares about. The boots might not fit you perfectly, but they'll probably suffice until we can get you some new ones. I've fixed for us to visit your school on Friday so we'll have a shopping excursion in Perth afterwards and get you a hat and some boots,' he said casually.

They walked over to the stable yard and

Vicky saw two horses standing already saddled, a great black gelding that looked as tall as a house and a smaller chestnut mare.

Vicky muttered, 'I hope the smaller one is mine.'

Ross grinned wickedly. 'Yes, that's Fennel. She's as gentle as a lamb and I thought she'd match your hair.'

He disappeared into the stables and reappeared with a hat and a pair of boots. 'Try these for size.'

The hat was fine, the boots a bit large, but Vicky decided she could cope with them.

At first they trotted at a gentle pace, Ross holding the big horse, Storm, in check. Then when he had established that Vicky was comfortable and ready to move faster, he changed tempo to a canter. They cantered round the estate grounds and then he struck off up the hillside.

The surface was heather, broken by small tussocks of bracken, just showing the curled pale-green leaves of the new season's growth. When they reached the crest of the hill, Ross reined in his horse and they stood side by side looking over the panorama of hazy blue mountains, valleys and silent lochs. Sheep cropped the grass, lifting their heads to gaze with mild curiosity as Fennel blew down her nostrils and Storm whinnied gently.

Ross pointed with his riding-crop. 'All this will be purple with flowering heather and the bracken will be knee-high by high summer.' His eyes were warm and a smile lifted the corners of his mouth.

'It's a magnificent view. You really love this place, don't you?' Vicky said.

'Do you think you're going to like it and settle happily here?' Ross asked, stroking the long shining black silk of his horse's neck.

'I think so, it's already started to weave its spell over me,' Vicky replied.

'Feel up to a gallop, now?' he asked. 'You can give her her head. She's a very sedate lady, not like this fellow. He can be a bit wild.'

Vicky nodded, nudged Fennel's sides with her knees and leaned forward. The horse responded and they were off down the hill. The wind rushed past Vicky's cheeks, teasing stray strands of hair from the tight knot she had fastened it into. She felt a wave of exhilaration mount within her. She had forgotten how satisfying riding could be.

Ross waited just long enough to ascertain that she was quite safe and then let Storm go. The great creature soon caught up and overtook Fennel, his huge strides covering the ground at an amazing speed.

When she reached the path that led into the grounds, Ross was waiting for her. Storm was dancing from one foot to the other, nostrils flaring. Obviously he still had an excess of energy.

'You enjoyed that?' grinned Ross, surveying

67

the wild rose colour in her cheeks and the sparkle in her eyes.

'It was brill,' laughed Vicky, lapsing into school language in her excitement.

When they returned from their ride on the second morning, Ross was met by Murray, the groom. 'Master Ross, there's been a telephone call for you and they want you to ring straight back.'

'Damn,' said Ross and headed for the house at a brisk pace.

He always helped to unsaddle and brush down his horse and Vicky suspected he enjoyed doing it, hence the irritation.

Vicky and Murray worked side by side, Vicky with Fennel, Murray with Storm.

'Have you been here a long time, too, Mr Murray?' she asked, watching his hand wield the curry-comb with dexterity.

'Och aye, nearly thirty-five years. I came here straight from school. Never wanted to go anywhere else. It's a guid place to work,' he said in his soft Highland accent.

'Do you remember my father?' said Vicky wistfully.

'Aye. Nice enough young fellow. Should never have wed Miss Helen, though. Too gentle to handle her, he was,' Murray said bluntly.

'How do you mean?' Vicky asked, excited at the thought that perhaps she was going to hear something that might explain her father's actions.

'Weel, she was beautiful, but wayward. She needed firm handling. Like a strong-willed horse, ye ken. He was besotted with her, but she could twist him round her little finger and I got the impression her feelings for him weren't quite as strong as his, though I could have been mistaken. But there was no mistaking the rows they had before he left. Everybody knew about them.'

'Have you finished with Storm, Murray?' Ross had somehow entered without them hearing him and Vicky suspected he'd overheard some of their conversation and wasn't pleased about it. He sounded curt and his face looked grim.

As they walked back to the house, he said shortly, 'Vicky, please don't gossip with the staff, it's not good form.'

Vicky said nothing, embarrassed at being caught trying to elicit information about his parents.

The school Ross had chosen for her was a small private one on the outskirts of Perth. When he drew up in front of the porticoed entrance, Vicky whispered, 'Ross, this will be frightfully expensive, surely ? I thought I was just going to the local comprehensive.'

'It's not so expensive and in any case you'll only be here for half a term. It's where the local young ladies go. I thought this would be much better than plunging you into a huge

69

school where you'd just be a cipher. You'll get to know everyone easier here and they're prepared to tailor your studies to suit your needs. Come on and meet Miss Ewing, the head.'

Vicky liked her. She was obviously impressed by Ross. Vicky realised how ridiculous she had been to expect him to deposit her in a local authority school; obviously he had a standing to maintain in the district. Miss Ewing assured him that they would do everything possible to make Vicky's stay there a happy one. She was shown round the school, though there were no pupils, of course, they were on their Easter vacation.

Afterwards they drove into Perth, had lunch at an hotel and went on their shopping expedition. In spite of Vicky's protests that she had sufficient money of her own, Ross insisted on paying for her purchases and she ended up with several dresses, a riding-habit, boots and hat, and the most exquisite evening dress in midnight-blue taffeta. Ross had chosen it, whilst informing her that she would need it for a ball they would shortly be attending.

He deviated on the return journey and took her to see Loch Tay, silvery beautiful in the spring sunshine, and showed her Scone Palace, saying, 'You'll have to come and visit it, it's where all the Scottish kings were crowned until Charles II in 1651. It's closed now; they open at Easter, like us.'

It had been a perfect day and when Ross dropped her off at the side entrance with her parcels, Vicky wandered in with a happy smile on her face. The smile was soon removed. Alison appeared and said sharply, 'Oh, you have returned at last. Is Ross with you? I've been waiting for him to sign some letters for hours. I thought you would be back at lunchtime.'

Vicky flushed at the condemning tone in Alison's voice and the barely suppressed fury in her eyes.

'He's parking the car. I don't know about us being expected back for lunch. Ross just said we were eating out,' Vicky explained patiently, not wanting to get into a heated discussion with Alison.

'I suppose he thinks he has to chauffeur you around. He's a soft touch, collects passengers and parasites without trying; but I'm telling you we can't afford to carry passengers here, there's too much to be done to make a success of this place,' Alison warmed to her theme.

Vicky felt a cold anger mounting within her at the cruel words, but she replied softly, 'I'm not sure who you mean when you refer to passengers and parasites. Me, perhaps?'

'Oh, you and several others. Sir Malcolm, who ought to be in a nursing home and who takes up so much of Ross's time. A host of old retainers, who ought to be pensioned off to make way for some new blood. And now a

71

half-sister he didn't even know he had.' Alison's face was almost contorted with the malevolence she obviously felt.

Vicky took a long, shaky breath and fought for control before saying, 'Listen to me, Miss MacLeod. It wasn't my idea to come here. I had a perfectly good home in Cornwall and was quite prepared to stay there. It was Ross who insisted on uprooting me and bringing me here.'

'Oh quite. That's just what I mean. His damned over-developed sense of duty again,' Alison said dismissively, then added viciously, 'And now you listen to me. Ross and I go back a long way, do you get my meaning? And I intend eventually to become Mrs Cameron. When that happens you won't be welcome here—understand.'

Vicky looked bleakly at her and felt a cold lump of misery settle in her chest. 'Oh yes, I get your meaning all right. You needn't worry—if you ever become mistress here it would be the last place I'd want to stay.'

Vicky turned away and held her head high, determined that Alison should not see how upset she was. She went quickly to her room, hugging her parcels to her aching chest. The brightness and happiness had all gone from the day. Dispersed by a few cruel and well-chosen words from Alison MacLeod.

The phrase 'we go back a long way' kept running round in Vicky's head. What did

Alison mean? That she and Ross had been; or still were lovers? The thought filled Vicky with despair. She dropped her parcels on the floor, no longer interested in her lovely new possessions, and threw herself down on the bed in the sanctuary of her room and let the pent-up tears flow.

CHAPTER FIVE

When her tears were exhausted, Vicky got up from the bed. She looked at herself in the mirror of the dressing-table and winced. Her eyes were red and puffy from weeping. In short, she looked a mess. She went into the pretty pink and gold en-suite bathroom and bathed her eyes with cold water, showered and then started methodically to unpack her parcels and hang the clothing in the large cupboards. She hesitated with one dress in her hand and then dropped it onto the bed. 'I might as well wear it, it might improve my appearance a bit. It certainly needs it,' Vicky muttered to herself. The dress was silk, in misty shades of green and blue. The skirt was full, clinched with a wide black belt at the waist, and it flared in a blur of colour around her calves when she walked. It had long, full sleeves, dropping from softly gathered shoulders. It flattered her, Vicky had to admit.

She left her hair loose, but concentrated on applying make-up to cover up the ravages of her tears, using a greeny-blue eyeshadow more generously than she usually did.

Ross greeted her gaily when she appeared at the foot of the stairs. 'I wondered where you'd disappeared to. Been gloating over your new wardrobe, have you? You look lovely in that dress, it was definitely meant for you.'

As if suddenly aware of her silence he looked hard at her. 'What's the matter. You look upset or tired. Was it too much for you?' He looked concerned now.

'No, no, of course not. It was a lovely day. Thank you so much. And for the lovely clothes. But Ross—' Vicky hesitated, not knowing quite how to say what she felt she should. 'You mustn't feel you have to spend a lot of time on me and take me about. You're busy, I know. I'm sorry if I kept you from your work, today.' Vicky floundered to a halt, wondering if she had said too much.

'What the hell are you talking about, Vicky? Today was entirely my idea and I thoroughly enjoyed it. I do deserve and take time off occasionally, you know.'

Vicky had looked away when she finished her little diatribe. Now Ross moved towards her and took her chin in his hand and gently, but firmly turned her face so that he could look at her. She felt his grey eyes searching hers, as if to read the truth there, and she veiled them with the sweep of long lashes.

He said softly, 'Who's been getting at you? You've been crying, haven't you? Or perhaps I don't need to ask. Did you bump into Alison as you came in?'

Vicky remained silent. There seemed no point. in admitting it. If what Alison said was the truth, nothing Ross said would make any difference to the way she felt. She wondered whether he was in love with Alison and whether that blinded him to her maliciousness. She thought about what she'd said about Sir Malcolm and knew that Ross would be angry and hurt, he was very fond of his grandfather. She supposed she could have repeated what Alison had said, but she would have gained very little satisfaction. It would only have hurt Ross and that was the last thing she wanted to do. If he was involved with Alison it would cause him pain to know how she felt about people he was fond of, so Vicky said nothing.

Ross shook his head and said roughly, 'Damn her. You shouldn't let her needle you. She doesn't mean half she says. Her bark's worse than her bite. She seemed to think I'd said I'd be back at lunchtime. I'm sure I never did. Don't let it worry you. She'll get over it. Come on, let's go and eat. Grandfather will think we've abandoned him.'

Nothing more was said about the incident. and Vicky tried to push it from her mind, but she determined to steer clear of Alison as much as possible. And every time she thought about the possibility of Ross marrying Alison, she felt a dull pain somewhere in her chest.

The following day she took her sketch-pad and headed for one of the hills that overlooked the Hall. She wanted to try to get a bird's eye view of it. She worked hard, completely absorbed in her work, all afternoon and was just putting the finishing touches to it when she became aware that she was being watched. She turned her head to see who it was and was startled and felt her pulse quicken in alarm at the strange figure that stood in the shadow of a tree, watching her. She looked like some sort of witch. She had on a long rusty-black skirt and a tattered tartan plaid was draped around her thin bony shoulders. Her hair was grey and wispy and trailed round her face like cobwebs. The face itself was gaunt with deep eye-sockets, but the eyes within were black and gleamed like bright bits of jet. Vicky felt a shudder run down her spine. There was something strangely menacing about the odd figure.

She muttered something in an unknown tongue, that Vicky took to be Gaelic, and edged forward to where Vicky sat, her black eyes fixed on the painting.

'Ye're his daughter, aren't ye? Tremayne's. Ye're like him and ye have his talent. He was kind to puir old Meg. Always had a word when he saw me. They said cruel things about him, but I knew better.' She mumbled on, lapsing into Gaelic again.

Vicky felt her fears subside. She was just a poor, muddled old crone, but she obviously knew something about Vicky's father. Vicky sought to recapture the woman's attention. 'Yes, I am his daughter, Victoria. You say you knew my father. Do you know what happened? Why he went away?'

'Used to ride up here on that great beast of hers, she did. Thought no-one knew where she went, but old Meg knew. Used to meet the dark one at the bothy, up on the hill, she did. Thought old Meg was simple, everyone does, but I've sharp eyes that see more than some folk think.' She cackled with laughter, showing toothless gums, a weird sound that chilled Vicky's blood. She glanced up at the ruin on the hill with her strange, black, blank eyes.

Vicky had to know, had to be sure who she meant. 'Who do you mean? Who used to ride to the bothy?' she asked quickly, wanting to keep the old woman's mind from straying.

'Miss Helen, of course. She who married your father. Bewitched him, she did. Bad for him, she was.' She was mumbling to herself again.

'Who did she meet at the bothy?' persisted Vicky, feeling an excitement run through her at the thought that she might find something to justify her father's apparent desertion of his

77

wife.

'The dark one, that's who she met. Used to ride from the castle and wait for her, he did.'

'Is that all you know about him?' Vicky asked, disappointed that no name had been mentioned.

'Long time ago. Meg gets muddled. Noises in her head. Voices of people long gone away.' The old woman sounded peevish and moved her head restlessly, as if wanting to shake away the remembrances of the past. Then she suddenly turned those strange black eyes, in their deep shadowy sockets and gazed into Vicky's eyes. She clutched at Vicky's arm with long bony fingers that reminded Vicky of talons and said, 'Ye and he, Master Ross. His daughter, her son, ye two together will banish the dark secret.'

She turned and hurried down the hill, a strange bent figure, with her skirts and the ancient plaid flapping in the breeze, like some old scarecrow.

Vicky glanced at her watch. The light was fading. She'd been out longer than she had intended. She started packing up her easel and paints. Ross had said something about going out to dinner. She tried to remember if he'd said where they were going, but her head was buzzing with the strange encounter with the old woman called Meg and her even stranger remarks. She puzzled about what she could mean about she and Ross banishing the 'dark secret'. She supposed they had, in a way, by meeting and becoming friends.

She started to make her way down the hill, back to the Hall, trying to hurry, but hampered by her easel and painting equipment. She glanced back at the old ruined bothy at the top of the hill and determined that she would climb to the top of the hill next time and see if the bothy housed any evidence of those secret meetings between Helen and the mysterious dark man. Not that she was too hopeful, it looked little more than a ruin now. As things turned out it was to be several weeks before Vicky made her trip to the bothy.

She was hot and thirsty when she reached the Hall and, dropping her painting gear in the hallway, she stuck her head round the kitchen door and asked. ' 'Any chance of a cup of tea, Mrs Thompson? I'm dying of thirst.'

'Oh, Miss Vicky, where have you been? Master Ross was looking for you,' she said worriedly, but she was already pouring a cup of tea and cutting a large slice of fruity Dundee cake for Vicky.

Vicky sat at the kitchen table, munching cake and drinking tea and eventually managed to explain her absence. 'I was painting halfway up the hill there, and it took me longer than I'd expected, then this strange old woman appeared. Meg, her name was. She remembered my father. Fancy that, after all this time.'

'Old Meg Macgregor it would be. She's simple, always has been. And there's nothing strange about her remembering things that happened thirty years ago. She can do that, but she canna remember things she's done yesterday,' Mrs Thompson said dryly. Then she continued, 'She lives in a tumbledown old cottage at the edge of the estate. Master Ross has been trying for years to persuade her to let him have it repaired and modernised, but she'll no' have any of it. Will no' let anyone past the door.'

'Did Ross's mother ride a horse? She said she used to ride up the hill to the bothy. It looks as if it's just a ruin now,' Vicky said, wondering if Mrs Thompson would volunteer any more information.

'Och aye, Miss Helen was a bonny horsewoman. Used to ride a great black horse, a bit like that great brute of Master Ross's. I was always terrified she'd get thrown, the way she used to gallop across the countryside, but she never did. I think she had used to ride up to the bothy sometimes, but it's little more than a heap of stones, now.'

'Who lives in the castle at the far side of the loch, Mrs Thompson?' asked Vicky, curious to find out who the dark man was that Helen used to meet.

'Why Mr Abrahams, of course. That's where you're dining tonight. Didn't you know?'

'I think Ross did mention that we were having dinner with some people called Abrahams, but I didn't think to ask where they lived. Have they been there a long time.'

'Och no. Only about three years. Mr Abrahams owns a chain of hypermarkets, or somesuch, and is very wealthy. He bought the castle when it was little more than a ruin and had it completely rebuilt. More money than sense, I say. It was always a draughty old place. Must cost a fortune to heat and he's nae there half the time.' Mrs Thompson looked disgusted by these comparative strangers to the glen.

'Who owned it when my father was here?' Vicky asked, trying desperately not to sound too eager for the answer.

Mrs Thompson looked at her sharply, as if surprised that Vicky had brought her father into the conversation again. 'Och, it would be old Lord Kirriemuir. It was starting to fall into disrepair then. His lordship was over ninety when he died and had nae direct kin, so there was no-one to take over. It stayed empty for years and then some distant relatives of his, on the other side of the world, decided to put it on the market and eventually Mr Abrahams bought it.'

'Did Sir Malcolm and Miss Helen used to visit the castle?' Vicky asked, wondering how she could find out the identity of the mystery man. Obviously it wasn't Lord Kirriemuir if

81

he'd been so old.

Vicky never did get her question answered. Ross's voice, sharply accentuated, said, 'Are you going to sit there gossiping all evening, Vicky, or can I hope that you will get ready and accompany me to Kirriemuir Castle?'

Vicky blushed furiously. She had no idea how long Ross had been standing in the open doorway or how much of the conversation between Mrs Thompson and herself he had overheard. She stammered, 'I—I'm sorry, Ross. I'll get changed now. I was thirsty after being out all afternoon and asked Mrs Thompson for some tea.'

'You could have told me where you were going, then I wouldn't have wasted time searching the grounds for you.' His tone was mild, but with an underlying hint of steel.

'I'm sorry. You seemed busy and I wanted to paint the house from the hill. I didn't intend to be out so long.' Vicky thought she seemed to be doing nothing but stammer apologies.

She hurried out of the kitchen, followed closely by Ross. 'Thanks for the tea, Mrs Thompson,' she called back.

Ross closed the kitchen door firmly and then laid his hand on her arm, preventing her from making for the stairs. 'Come into my study for a moment, will you, Vicky?'

Vicky glanced anxiously at his face and was not reassured. His mouth was set in a thin line and his expression was grim, to say the least.

Vicky trailed miserably towards the door of the study. She had never been in there before.

Ross ushered her in and gestured to a chair near his desk. She had a brief impression of books and a large, carved oak desk, before she spotted her sculpture sitting on the desk. She felt a little thrill of pleasure to think that he had put it on his desk, knowing he spent quite a lot of time in this room. She had wondered what he had done with it, but hadn't liked to ask.

She forgot his displeasure and said eagerly, 'That's where you put my sculpture, then?'

'Yes, it looks good, doesn't it?' His tone was slightly warmer. It was short-lived.

'Vicky, do you remember me asking you not to discuss my parents with the staff?' he said bluntly.

'I didn't mean to. It was just that this old character—Meg—came up to me and said she remembered my father and went on about your mother. I'm sorry, but I was curious,' Vicky said apologetically, but then continued more defensively, 'She said my father was kind to her. She didn't condemn him.'

'Vicky, she's a poor muddled simpleton. Always was. I wouldn't take what she says too seriously,' Ross said, more sympathetically.

'Yes, well perhaps you're right, but I still feel there's something odd about it all,' Vicky persisted.

Ross was angry now. 'I don't know what

you're trying to prove, Vicky, but for God's sake leave it alone and stop prying. Nothing good can come of it now, it's all ancient history. They're both dead, leave them in peace. Don't you realise what you're trying to do? You're trying to justify my father's behaviour by trying to find something with which to discredit my mother. How's that going to help me?'

Vicky looked shaken and tears filled her eyes at the harshness of his tone. She said slowly, 'I'm sorry. I really never thought of that aspect. I think it might have been better if I hadn't come here.'

'Vicky, love, don't say that. I enjoy having you here and you've been settling in so well. Just concentrate on being happy here and forget the past, will you?' he said gently.

Vicky nodded. 'Yes, of course. I won't ask any more questions.'

'Good girl. Go and make yourself look pretty now.'

Vicky dressed herself in the long black velvet skirt and white ruffled blouse and put her hair up on top of her head, wondering what this Mr Abrahams would be like and whether he had a family. She picked up a tartan cloak that Ross had bought her on their shopping jaunt and went to join him.

'I'm glad to see you have something warm to wear. It will be cool on the loch, particularly when we're coming back,' Ross said, taking her arm.

Vicky stiffened. 'W—what did you say about the loch?'

'Oh, didn't I tell you? We're going by boat. It's much quicker. It's a long tortuous road all round the loch. By boat, it's straight across the loch and Sim Abrahams is going to send a car down to the landing-stage to meet us at the other side,' Ross said unconcernedly.

Vicky turned panic-stricken eyes upon him and gasped, 'Ross, I can't do it. I can't go on water on a boat. The thought terrifies me.'

Ross clasped a hand to his forehead and said, 'God, what a fool I am. I never thought about how you might feel about boats. I'd forgotten about the accident. I'll have to ring Sim and tell him we'll be late. It will take much longer by car.'

Vicky looked miserable. 'I'm sorry, Ross, for messing up your plans. Why don't you go without me? I don't mind, honestly.'

'Silly girl. It's you they want to meet.' Ross hesitated, then put both hands on her shoulders and turned her so that he could look right into her face. 'Vicky, I won't push you, but don't you think it might be worth trying to conquer your fear? Remember your nightmare? It went away, didn't it, after you talked about it? Don't you think this might be the same? You know what they tell someone who's been in a car crash to do—get back in and drive again as quickly as possible. The loch is as calm as a millpond, you know. Not like the sea. And we're going by motor launch, not using sail. It couldn't be safer. It's probably safer than going by car.'

Vicky thought about it. Her logic told her he was right. She couldn't go on avoiding water travel indefinitely, particularly if she wanted to see much of Scotland. Unfortunately a part of her brain clung to her unreasonable fear.

She looked at Ross, her eyes mirroring her nervousness, and said stiffly, 'I'll try, but you'll have to bear with me if I suddenly go to pieces.'

He took her hand and squeezed it. 'That's my girl. You'll be safe with me. I'll see no harm comes to you.' He gave her a reassuring smile.

Vicky almost froze as Ross handed her into the boat, but with a quiet word of encouragement, she made it.

'Do you want to go into the cabin? It will be warmer,' Ross asked, eyeing her pallid face with concern.

'No, I want to stay as close to you as possible. I don't want to be on my own, where my imagination can run riot. Keep talking to me, please,' Vicky begged.

Ross laughed, but helped her over to the helm, after casting off. Vicky stood very close to him, finding the warmth from his body a comfort. After he'd cleared the landing-stage, he slipped one arm round her shoulders and steered one-handed, pointing out landmarks and chatting easily. Vicky found her fears subsiding and even managed to enjoy the last, few minutes of the trip.

The car was waiting, as promised, and they were soon whisked up to the castle. Simeon Abrahams was waiting for them. He was a small, plump, effusive man of Jewish descent. His head was bald and his face crumpled up into folds of flesh when he smiled, which he did constantly. With his innocent blue eyes he reminded Vicky of a chubby baby. Ross had told her that he was a hard-headed businessman, completely ruthless when it came to clinching a money-making deal in his favour, so his looks were obviously deceptive.

He led the way into a vast, imposing dining-room and introduced them to his wife, a small, plump, pretty woman with a quantity of dark, wavy hair, and his son, Daniel. The son, by contrast, was thin and shy, with a crop of spots. Vicky thought he must be about eighteen. He blushed furiously when introduced to Vicky and then stared at her as if unable to take his eyes away.

Vicky thought they were probably in for a rather odd evening and Ross, obviously guessing her thoughts, raised a quizzical eyebrow and winked.

As they were being seated at the long dining-table, he leaned towards her and whispered, 'I think poor Daniel is rather smitten,' and his lips twitched in amusement.

Vicky frowned at him, irritated by his obvious amusement. She couldn't quite understand the ambiguity of her feelings. She wanted Ross's friends to like her, but she wanted Ross to be a little jealous of the obvious interest Daniel was showing towards her. The fact that Ross found it funny piqued her.

She deliberately set out to charm Daniel, exerting herself to talk to him and put him at his ease. Daniel blossomed under her kindness and by the time they reached the dessert stage, she had not spoken a word to Ross, sitting on her other side. Simeon had been doing most of the talking to Ross, telling him of various business deals. As he got up to replenish their wine-glasses, Ross took the opportunity to whisper in Vicky's ear, 'Am I getting the cold-shoulder treatment? Have I upset you in some way?'

Vicky gave him a brilliant smile and murmured, 'Of course not, whatever gave you that idea?'

Ross shrugged. 'You seem to have ignored me all evening. I thought perhaps you were still put out by my comments to you earlier.'

'I'm not at all put out. I'm only being sociable to your friends. Besides, you can talk to me any time,' Vicky replied airily.

'Yes, well watch what you're doing with Daniel. He's not used to attractive young females exerting their charms on him. He's rather impressionable, I think,' Ross said dryly.

Mrs Abrahams was warmly friendly towards Vicky and told her she must come over to the castle any time she liked. That it would be nice for Daniel to have company of his own age. Vicky gathered that she was pleased that Daniel had overcome his initial awkwardness.

Vicky thanked her, but pointed out that she would be going to school after Easter and was busy preparing for her A-levels, so would have little spare time. Daniel was all right, but Vicky didn't feel they had a lot in common and she didn't want him to harbour hopes she couldn't fulfil. He seemed so very young and gauche, somehow. She realised that the boys she had known in Cornwall seemed very young now, as well, in retrospect. She suspected that she had grown up a great deal in the short time since her parents' deaths. She realised, too, that she now tended to compare other males with Ross and they all seemed to pale into insignificance by comparison.

The thought alarmed her a little. She wondered whether she would ever find anyone who measured up to him. She had known him so little time and yet he seemed to dominate her thoughts and she couldn't imagine being without him now.

CHAPTER SIX

Good Friday dawned sunny and warm. Drumorchy Hall was a hive of activity in preparation for the expected rush of visitors. Most of the staff were part-time and casual workers from the nearby villages.

Vicky wondered where she could best help. She had meant to ask Ross what he would like her to do, but she didn't seem to have seen much of him over the past few days. He had been rushing round, organising everything, often with Alison in tow, so Vicky had given them a wide berth.

She wandered towards the office, where she was bumped into by Alison who was rushing out of the door with a pile of guide books clutched in her arms.

'I hope you're not going to get under everyone's feet, Vicky. We're all too busy to entertain you and Ross certainly won't want to be bothered by you,' she snapped shortly.

'I don't need entertaining and I was only trying to find Ross to ask him where I could best help,' Vicky replied, striving to keep a hold on her temper. She realised if it came to a battle of words between Alison and herself, she would probably be the loser. Alison's tongue was like a rapier.

'The best thing you can do is to take

yourself off somewhere out of the way until all the visitors have gone home.' Alison flicked a derisive look at Vicky and headed across the hall.

'Thank you, and a pleasant day to you, too,' Vicky shouted sarcastically after her retreating back.

She decided to go and see how Sir Malcolm was faring. She knocked on the door of his little private sitting-room, rightly deducing that he would hide himself there whilst the house was being invaded by visitors.

At his instruction to enter, she peeped round the door and said, 'I thought I'd come and see how you were and if you'd like some company.'

'I'd love some company and I'm feeling bloody useless,' he said gruffly.

'You and me both, then,' said Vicky ruefully.

He looked surprised. 'You useless, what nonsense.'

Vicky gave a mirthless laugh. 'So I've just been told by Alison. I've been instructed to keep out of the way.'

He snorted. 'I shouldn't take too much notice of what she says. If she can't file you or make money from you, she's at a loss to know what to do with you.'

Vicky laughed and felt better. She seated herself beside him and said, 'What would you like to do to take your mind off the milling hordes? You hate it all, don't you?' She looked at him sympathetically.

He nodded. 'Yes, I can never reconcile myself to having my home walked all over by perfect strangers, even though I recognise the necessity. Let's play a game of chess.'

He was good at chess. He might be physically handicapped, but his brain was still astute and he beat Vicky easily in their first game. Vicky realised that her mind was not entirely on the game, she was thinking about Ross. He'd cried off their early morning ride, saying he had too much to do, so she hadn't seen him since dinner the previous evening.

She tried to concentrate a little more during their second game and was faring better, when they were interrupted by Mrs Thompson bringing Sir Malcolm's coffee.

'So this is where you are, Miss Vicky. I wondered where you'd disappeared to after breakfast.'

'Well I tried to offer my services, but they were rejected rather forcefully, so I thought I'd keep Sir Malcolm company,' Vicky explained wryly.

'What did you want to do?' asked Mrs Thompson.

'I didn't mind. Anything that was needed. But I couldn't find Ross and Alison more or less told me to get lost.'

'Hmph, she would,' said Mrs Thompson and she and Sir Malcolm exchanged knowing looks.

'They're short-handed at the café. One of the women who was coming to help sent a message this morning to say her little boy had measles and she couldn't leave him. I don't know whether you feel like helping there?' Mrs Thompson looked uncertain.

'I wouldn't mind at all,' Vicky said enthusiastically.

'Well have your coffee first. There is a spare cup and saucer in Sir Malcolm's cupboard and there's plenty of coffee in the pot.'

Vicky drank her coffee with Sir Malcolm and then he said, 'Thank you for keeping an old man company. I think I'll have a little rest now. We'll leave our chess game and finish it another time.'

Vicky slipped out by the side entrance, not wanting to encounter Alison again, and walked quickly down the path that led to the café and souvenir shop. She'd met Mrs Finlay, a large, friendly lady who was in charge of the café, and thought she could work with her quite amicably.

'I hear you're short-handed, can I be of any help?' she asked.

'Bless you, yes, Miss Vicky. We could certainly use another pair of hands,' Mrs Finlay said cheerfully.

There were two young girls helping her, one who was on holiday from school, but the café was busy. People were just coming in for mid-morning coffee. Vicky was co-opted to clear and wipe tables and then later she helped to replenish the glass cabinets that housed the sandwiches and cakes. She didn't bother going back to the house for lunch. She stayed and had some with Mrs Finlay, Anne and Heather. They all got on well together and discovered they made a good team.

The house and grounds closed at five and the café was empty. The day had flown and Vicky felt tired, but satisfied. She felt at least she had been some use. She was scraping the scraps of food from plates and rinsing the excess off cutlery and china, before stacking the large dish-washer with washing-up, when she heard Ross's voice.

He was talking to Mrs Finlay, asking how she'd coped. Vicky continued working, although she flushed with pleasure when she heard Mrs Finlay say what a help she had been to them. She was just bending down to get another waste-bucket when Ross's voice said, very close to her, 'What on earth do you think you're doing labouring here? I wondered where you'd hidden yourself when you didn't join me for lunch.'

'I've enjoyed working here and at least I feel useful and people here are nice to me,' Vicky said rather defensively.

'Meaning?' said Ross, a little brusquely.

'Well I was told to keep out of the way. I felt a nuisance and unwelcome,' Vicky mumbled, regretting her little outburst. It really wasn't

Ross's fault if he had a shrew for a secretary and he had enough on his mind, without her adding to his worries.

He frowned. 'Oh I suppose you and Alison have been having another spat. What is it with you two?'

'I don't know. I don't try to antagonise her, but she seems to resent my presence here. She appears to be possessive about you and doesn't like my taking up any of your time,' Vicky explained miserably.

'Are you sure you're not being over-sensitive?' Ross asked gently, but obviously thinking Vicky was exaggerating the situation.

Vicky flushed angrily. 'No, I'm not being over-sensitive. She's rude to me every time she sees me. I'm sorry if you think I'm somehow to blame, but I don't know what I can do about it, short of keeping out of her way, which was what I was doing this morning,' Vicky muttered through stiff lips. She could feel tears very near and didn't want to let Ross see how his words had hurt her.

Mrs Finlay came into the kitchen at that juncture, so Ross didn't pursue the matter. Instead he said, 'Come on now and have a rest before dinner.'

'Thank you, dear, you were a great help,' said Mrs Finlay, obviously unaware of the tension in the air.

Vicky replied, 'I enjoyed it and I shall come to help each day until I start school,' sending

Ross a defiant look, as if daring him to forbid her to do so. But he merely raised an eyebrow and grinned resignedly.

The following day they ran short of change in the café and Mrs Finlay asked Vicky if she would run up to the office to get some. Alison and Ross were there when Vicky made her request and Alison said, so pleasantly that Vicky's mouth dropped open, 'Hello, Vicky, I hear you're being a great help at the café. Ross tells me that you were upset yesterday by some little remark of mine. You'll have to forgive me, I was rather harassed at the time. Am I forgiven?' Her back was towards Ross and, although her words sounded as sweet as honey, there was a look of' dislike in the eyes that were turned towards Vicky.

Vicky hesitated, not knowing what to say in the face of such hypocrisy, and Alison turned to Ross, her eyes soft and distressed, and said with a catch in her voice, 'You see, I've said I'm sorry, but I don't think Vicky wants to be friends with me.'

Vicky gulped at the slyness of Alison's tactics, for Ross was watching her, waiting for her reaction. She said stiffly, 'Yes, of course I'll forgive you and I'm only too happy to be friends with you.' She hoped she would be forgiven for the untruth, but she supposed she had better make the effort for Ross's sake.

'There you are, darling. I told you you were fussing about nothing,' said Alison triumphantly to Ross. 'You see, it was all a storm in a teacup.'

'I'd better get back with the change. Mrs Finlay was waiting for it,' Vicky said quickly, wanting to escape from Alison's cloying presence. She realised ruefully that she had just lost that round to Alison, too. If she ever complained to Ross again, he would be sure to think it was her fault, not Alison's.

The Hall didn't open on Sundays and Mondays. Ross had insisted on keeping Sunday free to spend as he liked and he devoted Mondays to estate matters. So on Easter Sunday Ross and Vicky breakfasted together and then went to the village church for the Easter service.

The spring blossom was just opening, that much later than in Cornwall, and Vicky thought back to the day of her parents' funeral when she had first met Ross.

When they returned from church, Ross suddenly said, 'Close your eyes, I have a surprise for you.'

Doing as she was instructed, Vicky found herself led round the Hall towards the yard by the garages and then was told to open her eyes. A new silvery-blue Metro stood there and Ross handed her a set of keys. Vicky looked amazed. 'What's this all about?'

'It's your birthday present. Get in and we'll try it out.'

'But it's not my birthday for another three

97

weeks and you can't really be giving me a car for it,' Vicky said incredulously.

'I am and I'm giving it to you early so that you can get used to it before you start school. You'll be able to drive yourself to and from Perth, then,' Ross smiled.

'Ross, it's super; you're too generous.' Vicky hurled herself at him and hugged him, murmuring incoherent thanks.

He laughed and squeezed her playfully. 'Come on, get in, you can take me for a drive in it to convince me you can handle it.'

Vicky felt shaky inside and she wasn't sure that it was all due to excitement over the car; she thought some of it was the result of being in contact with Ross's muscular body.

She drove round the lanes and into the village, getting used to handling the car, with Ross sitting silently beside her, until he pronounced himself satisfied. Then they returned to the Hall for lunch.

The following Saturday was the night of the ball. It was to be held at a large hotel and was considered quite an event. The proceeds were for charity and it was patronised by all the wealthy and important folk of the district. Vicky was excited about it and she thought of wearing her beautiful new gown. The only drawback seemed to be that Alison was going, too.

Ross was waiting for her in the hall when Vicky drifted down the stairs, the taffeta of her dress rustling as she walked. She caught her breath when she saw him, he looked so handsome in full Highland dress of Cameron kilt and black velvet jacket, with lace at neck and wrists. He looked as if he had stepped straight out of one of his ancestral portraits.

She watched his eyes warm as they took in her appearance, the blue of the dress deepening her eyes and the low neckline showing creamy shoulders. 'You look very beautiful,' he murmured appreciatively.

'So do you,' she blurted out breathlessly and then blushed.

Ross chuckled. 'I'm not sure whether beautiful can be applied to a man, but thank you all the same.'

'Well handsome, then, but you look so splendid. I feel as if I've stepped back into the pages of history. What's the dagger in your sock for?'

'Not a dagger, you ignorant child—a "skean-dhu",' Ross corrected laughingly, 'and it's all part of the Scottish ceremonial dress, but originally it would have been used as a weapon.'

'To bump off your enemies, when skulking in the heather, I suppose,' teased Vicky.

They were collecting Alison as they went through the village and once she was established in the rear seat, Vicky found herself growing silent as Alison monopolised the conversation.

She and Alison went to the cloakroom together to hand in their wraps and Vicky glanced quickly at her, not wanting to make it obvious that she was curious to see what the Scottish girl was wearing. Vicky was surprised by her appearance. She had expected Alison to be clad in something very sophisticated, but she wasn't. She was wearing a white dress with a full skirt and a sash in her clan tartan was fastened at her shoulder. The outfit made her look strangely innocent and when Vicky saw her standing near Ross her spirits plunged. They looked so right together, the simplicity of Alison's dress complementing the richness of Ross's attire. She realised as she looked around the ballroom that many girls were wearing white dresses. The men in their kilts of varied shades were the butterflies and the girls were snowy flowers, she thought, wondering if she were over-dressed.

She soon discovered that a lot of the dances were Scottish ones and she couldn't do them. She stood and watched as Ross took Alison in an eightsome reel and as they whirled together, with Alison laughing up into Ross's face, she felt excluded from the gaiety. Ross had introduced her to some friends of his and she stood chatting to them and later she didn't lack for partners in the dances that she could do. She even let herself be coaxed into trying a simple reel by a young man called Ian Robertson. She quite enjoyed it and was assured by Ian that with some practice she would make quite a creditable Scottish dancer.

She saw very little of Ross during the first half of the evening and began to wonder whether she was expected to make her own way into supper, but then he suddenly appeared and asked her for the supper dance, which was a waltz, and said that he would take her into supper. He was an excellent dancer and Vicky found it easy to follow him. Their steps fitted well together.

He looked down at her and said, 'You've been all right, haven't you? I could see you dancing. You even tried a Scottish dance, didn't you?'

'Well someone thought I was worth teaching,' Vicky said rather sharply and then realised how peevish she sounded. She hadn't meant to let Ross see that she was put out by his neglect of her.

'I'm sorry, I didn't realise I was neglecting you. You seemed to be enjoying yourself and I have various "duty dances" I have to do.'

'Oh I was fine, you needn't worry about me. I can look after myself,' she said carelessly.

'Mm, I wonder,' said Ross cryptically.

Vicky and Ross had just settled themselves at a table for supper when Alison appeared with a young man in tow.

'You don't mind if we join you, do you?" she said archly and proceeded to sit very close to Ross, ignoring the young man she'd been dancing with, and talking quietly to Ross and flirting with him, so that Vicky and Andrew were forced to talk to each other.

Vicky learned that he was a junior partner in a veterinary practice. He was nice, too nice for Alison, Vicky thought with a jaundiced opinion of Alison's character. She wondered whether he was keen on Alison and hurt by her cavalier treatment of him and her openly flirtatious manner with Ross, but he didn't appear to be bothered. He even said he would like to see Vicky again and asked if he could telephone her to arrange something and Vicky agreed. She realised that she had to make her own circle of friends in Scotland independently of Ross. She couldn't expect him to always include her in his engagements and activities and she told herself she hadn't to feel hurt when he excluded her.

Somehow Alison managed to appropriate the front passenger seat on the return journey, so Vicky was left by herself in the back. She made no attempt to join in the conversation, in fact she was tired and soon dozed off, not even realising when Alison was dropped off at her home. She was awoken by Ross shaking her and saying 'Come on, Cinderella. The ball's over and it's long past midnight. Time you were tucked up in bed.'

She struggled out of the car and discovered that one foot had gone to sleep and wouldn't support her. In fact she would have fallen had

Ross not slipped his arm round her and supported her until her foot was functional again.

'Did you enjoy the ball?' he asked.

'Oh, yes,' said Vicky and tried to instil a degree of enthusiasm into her voice, but inside she realised that her hopes for the ball hadn't been fulfilled; and yet if she had been asked what she had hoped for she would have been hard put to explain. Her feelings seemed to be in a very confused state, she thought ruefully, as she prepared for bed.

One bright spot in her new circumstances was her school. She had assured Ross that she was perfectly capable of driving herself to school and getting herself settled in, although he had wanted to take her on the first morning. She had overcome his doubts and had got herself to Perth and found the headmistress, who had introduced her to her new teachers and classmates. She had soon made friends and had been full of enthusiasm upon her return to the Hall, much to Ross's obvious relief.

Because she was away from Ross much of the day now, their relationship developed and became less intense. She had new friends who invited her out and visited her at the Hall. She had lots to talk about to Ross when she returned after school and they invariably chatted through dinner. They still rode together before breakfast, so they usually started and finished the day together.

An easy camaraderie developed between them and they teased each other and joked together as a brother and younger sister might have done.

Ross told her he had arranged to have a barbecue and dance for her eighteenth birthday and asked her to let him have a list of the guests she wanted inviting so that he could arrange to have invitations sent out. Vicky did so, including in her list friends from school and acquaintances of Ross's that she had met and liked. She deliberately left Alison off the list and waited to see if Ross would comment on the fact. He said nothing until after the invitations had gone out and then casually one day at breakfast said, 'I noticed you left Alison off your list of guests. Was it accidental or intentional?'

Vicky felt her face flame and was half tempted to say it had been an oversight, but then decided she might as well make a stand. She did not want Alison at her party and Ross might as well know now. Although Alison was scrupulously polite when Ross was present, she still made barbed remarks to Vicky when they were alone. The pretence of friendship was just a sham really.

She said carefully, trying to control the quiver in her voice, 'It was intentional. I'm sorry Ross, but I don't want Alison at my party. I've tried, but I can't really like her.'

Ross shrugged. 'Well it's your party so you must invite who you like. I just thought she might feel hurt if she was left out. I thought you two had agreed to a truce.'

'We did, but that doesn't mean we like each other any better. I don't think she'll expect to be invited,' Vicky said firmly, determined not to be coerced into inviting Alison.

Nothing more was said and Vicky was glad she had stood firm.

It was arranged that, weather permitting, the barbecue should be on the terrace, with the long French windows from the ballroom open, so that people could drift in and out.

Vicky anxiously surveyed the sky on the morning of her birthday, but the day looked set fair. They had been enjoying a warm, dry spell during May, but Vicky had been worried in case it changed and they had to move everything indoors; but her fears were unfounded, it was a perfect day for her birthday barbecue and dance.

Sir Malcolm had warned her that he would keep strictly to his rooms, muttering, 'I'm too old for that kind of junketing,' but his eyes had twinkled and his mouth had curved into his odd, lop-sided smile, so Vicky knew his fierceness was a sham.

They were all dressing casually, for the dancing was very informal. Vicky was wearing bib and brace type trousers in yellow cotton with a yellow and white striped shirt, and when she caught a glimpse of Ross he was attired in black cords and a white silk polo-necked shirt. Vicky thought he looked equally as handsome in casual attire as he had in formal dress.

He had given her a tiny parcel with his birthday card at breakfast-time and Vicky had discovered a box containing a fine gold chain, on which hung a pendant set with a perfect little pearl, her birthstone. She had protested that he had already given her a superb present in the form of her car and shouldn't have given her anything else.

Ross laughed and said, 'An eighteenth birthday is very important; I couldn't have let the day go by without marking it in some way.'

Vicky went to Sir Malcolm's room to say 'Goodnight' before the party began, as they weren't dining together in the usual way. He shook his head when he saw how she was dressed and said dryly, 'You young things! In my day a young lady's "coming of age" party would have been an excuse to dress herself in her most beautiful finery.'

Vicky wagged a finger at him and said teasingly, 'Ah, but remember I'm not really coming of age, am I? Ross is still in control until I'm twenty-one, isn't he? Perhaps I'll have a formal party then.'

He didn't reply to her comment; instead, he beckoned her over to where he sat at his writing-desk and said, 'Come here, I've got something for you.'

He handed her a small, square leather box and when she opened it, she discovered inside an exquisite antique gold ring, set with a large ruby.

Vicky stared in amazement. 'I can't accept this. It must be worth a lot of money,' she stammered.

'Of course you can accept it. It belonged to my wife and I had intended to give it to my daughter on her twenty-first birthday, but she never reached that age.' There was a break in his voice, before he continued, 'I'm giving it to you now, so that I can see you wearing it. I might not be around when you become twenty-one.'

'But what about Ross? Might he not want it for his wife, if it's a family heirloom?' Vicky protested.

'There's other jewellery he can give to his wife, that's if he ever gets round to marrying, but I want you to have this. This is my gift to you. You're a sweet-natured, kind-hearted girl.' Then he added vehemently, 'You must take after your mother.'

Vicky realised that he still hadn't forgiven her father, although he had never mentioned him again since that first day. She could no longer feel resentful towards him for his attitude, though, because she had come to like and respect him. She realised now how deep was his grief, even after all these years, over his daughter's death.

She bent down and kissed his lined cheek. 'Thank you, Sir Malcolm. I shall treasure it always.'

'Put it on then. Let me see how it looks,' he grunted.

She slipped the magnificent ring onto the fourth finger of her right hand and it glowed with a fiery redness. 'It looks a bit strange with my attire, but it's very beautiful.'

After bidding Sir Malcolm 'Goodnight,' she went in search of Ross to show him the ring and make certain that he didn't object to her accepting it. As she wandered out on to the terrace where Ross was checking on the barbecue, she thought again about Sir Malcolm's hatred of her father. She realised that she had been so busy over the past days that she had forgotten her resolve to visit the bothy to try to discover who the mysterious man was that Helen had met there. She was in a dilemma. Ross was right, of course; if she discovered anything to justify her father it would be at the expense of Helen and it would hurt Sir Malcolm to learn anything bad about his daughter. Whatever she discovered would have to be kept secret from him, she couldn't hurt him in any way; and possibly from Ross, too, since he grew so angry whenever the question of his parents' separation was mentioned. She knew, however, that she would have to try to find out whatever she could, for her own peace of mind.

She found Ross feeding charcoal on to the barbecue. 'Ross, your grandfather has just given me this ring.' She held out her hand and the glow from the burning charcoal made little flames dance from the ring. 'I told him I didn't want to accept it, that you might want to give it to your wife, when you marry, but he insisted.'

Ross glanced carelessly at the ring. 'Oh yes, it's the one grandmother was wearing when her portrait was painted. I don't object to his giving it to you. And what's this about my marrying. There's nothing to say I will and I certainly don't have any immediate plans.' There seemed to be an odd look about Ross's eyes as he looked at Vicky, which she couldn't understand, but she felt a surge of relief at his words. She was glad he had no immediate plans to marry, and although she realised the feeling was pure selfishness on her part, she didn't care.

CHAPTER SEVEN

Vicky had two days' holiday from school at the end of May and had decided to spend the first day completing her art folio. Since coming to Drumorchy Hall she had added a new section to it, based on Scottish architecture, using some of the old castles and manor houses of the district as her subjects.

She sat in a semi-secluded spot at the rear of the house, sketching the back view of the Hall and hoping the visitors wouldn't spot her. There appeared to be something fascinating about an artist at work and people always wanted to see what she was doing, a thing that embarrassed her greatly.

She was just putting the finishing strokes to the pen and ink sketch and congratulating herself on not being interrupted, when two American visitors wandered down the secluded little path.

'Gee look, Elmer, an artist. I must just see what she's drawing.' And the plump American lady rushed over to Vicky. Elmer followed more slowly, looking a little embarrassed at his wife's exuberance.

'Edie, honey, she might not want to be disturbed.'

Vicky smiled. One had to be polite to the visitors. It was good for publicity. 'It's all right. I've just finished, actually,' and she scrawled her name at the bottom.

'May we look? We just love this house. We think it's one of the cutest we've been to. Just like a real home,' Edie enthused.

Vicky subdued a wry smile. She could just imagine what Sir Malcolm's response would have been to a remark like that. 'Well I suppose so, but I'm not a professional artist, well not yet at any rate.'

But Edie was not deterred. She peered

eagerly at the sketch Vicky had made of the rear of the house and the herb garden that bordered it. 'Elmer, isn't that just the darlingest picture you've ever seen? I've just got to have it,' she cooed.

Vicky looked alarmed. 'But I don't really sell my pictures, not at present. I'm doing them for an art folio I have to complete.'

'Do you live here or are you just a visitor, too?' Elmer asked, his eyes shrewd behind thick-lensed glasses.

'I live here,' Vicky said in a puzzled voice, not quite seeing his line of reasoning.

'Well couldn't you do another one? I'm prepared to pay whatever you ask for it, if Edie wants it.' Obviously he was a man used to getting what he wanted.

'Well I suppose so,' Vicky said slowly, 'but I've no idea what to ask for it.'

'Fifty pounds?' he queried.

It sounded a lot to Vicky for an unframed sketch by an unknown artist and she felt quite flattered.

She nodded. 'All right then.'

'Are you related to Ross Cameron?' Edie asked, and then with a dreamy look. 'Isn't he just the loveliest man? He's just shown us round the inside of the Hall.'

Vicky wondered how much she should tell these strangers and then guardedly said, 'He's my half-brother.'

'Well isn't that just marvellous. Are you a

111

Cameron, too?' Then as she peered at Vicky's signature, 'Although your name is different.'

'No I'm not. It's all a bit complicated and I'd rather not go into the intricacies of the relationship, if you don't mind. We share the same father, but Ross is a Cameron from his mother's side.' Vicky stopped, wondering if she'd made matters even worse by her muddled explanation.

She could almost see the mental processes working in the heads of the two Americans, then Edie whispered in a conspiratorial fashion, 'Well, of course, I understand, my dear. Some of the relationships in these aristocratic families are very unorthodox, aren't they?'

Vicky blushed and felt sure now that Edie had come up with some weird and wonderful story for the manner in which she and Ross were related. She was so anxious to end the discussion that she practically thrust the drawing into Edie's hands.

Elmer withdrew a fat wallet from his inner pocket and extricated two twenty-pound notes and one ten-pound and pushed them into Vicky's hand.

'Thank you, honey. We shall treasure this. A bit of old Scotland hanging in our lounge. Of course we have Scottish connections, you know.'

'Haven't they all?' thought Vicky with amusement and wondered if she was to be treated to a history of the two Americans' ancestors, but fortunately the bell, signalling that visitors should leave because the grounds were being closed, started to toll at that moment.

Elmer and Edie hastened towards the exit, still thanking Vicky and waving their farewells. Vicky packed up her easel, stuffed the fifty pounds into her pocket and headed for the house.

She met Ross on the steps of the Hall. He raised his eyebrows and said, 'Phew, that was quite an afternoon. We've had this coachload of Americans all eager to "do" every scrap of Scotland they can cram into their itinerary. They never stopped asking questions.'

'I know, I've just met two of them. They've just talked me into selling a drawing I'd made of the rear of the house. I hope you don't mind, Ross. I never thought to ask if you objected to my selling it to them.'

'Of course not. It's probably good publicity, if they hang it on their wall and tell all their friends where they got it from. How much did they pay for it?' Ross asked.

'Fifty pounds. It seemed excessive to me for a pen and ink sketch, but it's what they offered. It only took me an hour or so to do it. I've never earned fifty pounds so easily,' Vicky laughed.

'I wouldn't be so sure it's excessive. When you're a famous artist that sketch will probably be worth far more than fifty pounds,' he said quite seriously.

Vicky chuckled with delight and patted his cheek affectionately. 'You are good for my ego, you know. I think I ought to give you the money; I'm sure they only bought it because you'd charmed them and they thought we were related.' She held the money out to him.

'Don't talk rubbish. Put it away and buy yourself something nice with it. I tell you what we could do, though. At the moment we only have picture postcards of the Hall for sale, but if we had your sketches copied and framed I bet they'd sell like hot cakes. How would you feel about it?' Ross said thoughtfully.

Vicky slipped her arm through his and hugged his arm to her side. 'Oh, Ross, what a simply splendid idea. I'd love that,' she said excitedly.

'Right, that's what we'll do then. I have to go to Edinburgh on business tomorrow. Whilst I'm there I'll make some enquiries about getting your drawings copied and printed.'

Ross set off early for Edinburgh the following day and Vicky, not wanting to run the risk of seeing Alison, decided it was a perfect occasion for making her trip up the hill to the bothy.

The weather was sunny and warm and the sky almost cloudless, so there was little chance of the mist, that sometimes hung about the summit, dropping. Vicky asked Mrs Thompson for some sandwiches for her lunch, telling her that she was going to do some sketching.

'Mind you take care, Miss Vicky, the last bit of the track is awful rough,' she warned, packing a flask and a large packet of sandwiches into a small rucksack.

Vicky soon arrived at the spot where she'd met the strange old woman, Meg, but from then on the climb became steeper and the path stonier. She wondered how Helen had managed it on a horse. Of course she could have ridden through the heather that flanked the path, that would probably be easier for a horse to negotiate than the bumpy stones, which occasionally came loose and rolled off down the hillside.

More than once she thought she had nearly reached the summit, but it was one of those deceptive hills with twists in the path and yet another hump to climb. She took to looking just at the path in front of her and counting slowly to one hundred, a trick she and her father had used when she was a child and they were out walking, in order to distract her from the distance she had to cover. At the thought of her father the old nagging pain of loss started up again inside and she quickened her pace. After all, this trip was on his behalf.

She realised with some surprise that she hadn't felt the loss of her parents so acutely in recent days and felt almost ashamed. She had been so involved in her new life that her former existence had become almost hazy.

She glanced up from her musings and was quite surprised to find that she was only a few feet from the top. She hurried the last bit and then flopped down on the sparse grass, breathless and with the beginnings of a stitch. She drew her knees up to her chin and looked down on the valley from whence she had just come.

Drumorchy Hall and the village looked like tiny models and the sheep and cows like the animals in a child's toy farm. The view was spectacular, though, and more than made up for the arduous climb. Soaring peaks of higher mountains like Schiehallion and Ben Lawers towered up into the azure of the sky and, below, the green spread of the valley was dotted with the deep aquamarine of lochs and silvery threads of rivers.

After drinking her fill of the view below, Vicky turned her gaze towards the bothy. An acute sense of disappointment descended upon her. She didn't know quite what she had expected; after all she had been warned that it was just a ruin. But she hadn't expected the crumbling heap of moss-covered stones that met her eyes. It was nothing but a shell. The roof had long since fallen in and the walls had long cracks and holes where stunted rowans and willow-herb clung and flourished with amazing tenacity.

A sharp lance of disappointment ran

through Vicky. She had hoped, foolishly perhaps, that some clue to the other partner in those long ago trysts might be found here, but it was obvious that any evidence would have disappeared in the constant wearing away by the elements.

Vicky shrugged, sat on a tussock of grass and got out her sketch-book. The bothy had a strange, barren beauty about it. She might as well make use of it and draw it whilst she was here, she thought.

Completing her sketch, she stood up, stretched and then ate her lunch. She was just about to retrace her steps down the hill when she decided she might just as well have a look inside and see what was left.

The door hung drunkenly on rusted hinges and groaned protestingly as Vicky opened it sufficiently to slip through. There was just one room with an earth floor, but someone had put down a rug of some sort. The pattern had disappeared for it was rotting and mildewed. There was also a wooden cot-like bed, also with damp, rotting coverings. Vicky supposed that originally the shepherd owner would have slept in the bothy when he was working with his sheep and didn't want to return to his home in the valley.

As she had seen from the outside, the roof had crumbled and the room was open to the sky. It was hard to tell whether there had been a proper fireplace and chimney, or just a bricked-in area with a hole in the roof for the smoke to go through. The stones around the fireplace were blackened with soot, and bits of charred wood lay there, telling of the fires that had once warmed the occupants.

Vicky wandered over and idly poked at a half-burnt log with her foot. It rolled over revealing some scraps of paper, yellowed with age and partially charred, but not completely devoured by the flames. Curious, she bent and picked up the scraps of paper. They were bits of a torn-up letter that someone must have thrown into the fireplace and tried to burn, but hadn't quite succeeded.

She smoothed the tattered pieces and tried to fit them together. Her eyes fell on the signature of the writer and her pulse quickened. In spite of the age of the letter, the signature said 'Helen' quite clearly. There were some other words above the signature; some were obviously incomplete or missing, but two words hit Vicky like hammer blows— 'love you'. So Helen had been seeing another man. Vicky tried to make something of the rest of the bits, with hands that shook. The letter was scrappy and disjointed and the name of the person to whom the letter had been sent was missing, but odd words gave her the gist of the letter: 'must see you', 'desperate', 'can't live without—' 'please come—' 'Friday afternoon—' The words told their own story. It was an impassioned plea for the mysterious dark man to meet her in the bothy, because she loved him so much that she couldn't live without him.

Vicky felt cold and shaky inside. 'Poor Daddy,' she whispered. 'He must have found out and that's why he left her.'

Vicky stuffed the scraps of paper in the pocket of her jeans and started to wend her way back down the hill. She didn't quite see how the information was going to help her in her quest to clear her father's reputation. She still didn't know who the man was and she realised she couldn't possibly confront Ross with the evidence of his mother's infidelity. It would hurt him too much. She realised that her motives had undergone a change. When she had arrived in Scotland she had been determined at all costs to find out the truth and vindicate her father. Now, she had grown so fond of Ross that even if the truth never came to light, there was no way that she could hurt him.

When she arrived at the Hall she was preoccupied with her thoughts and both Mrs Thompson and, later at dinner, Ross asked her if she was all right.

She made discreet and tentative enquiries over the next few weeks about who else might have visited the bothy besides Helen, but drew a complete blank and was reluctantly forced to admit that the mystery would probably remain unsolved.

The summer flew by. Vicky sat her A-levels and completed her stay at school. Ross took her back down to Cornwall to collect the remainder of her belongings and Edward Frost contacted her to say that an old friend of her father's, an artist, wanted to rent the house. He advised Vicky to accept and she did so, feeling that at least the house would still belong to her and that having an acquaintance living in it was preferable to a complete stranger.

August brought her results—good ones. Her place at college in Lancaster was assured. Term started at the beginning of October and she had a room in the hall of residence. She was eager to start on her art course and yet reluctant to leave Ross and Drumorchy Hall. She was confused by her conflicting emotions.

At the end of September they had an 'Indian summer' and the weather was unseasonably warm for Scotland. On the last Sunday in September, the day before Vicky's departure to Lancaster, Ross said, 'Let's take a picnic lunch and go to the loch. We could even have a bathe, it's warm enough.'

Vicky grimaced. 'Ugh, I bet the loch water will be freezing cold.' But she went off obediently to get her swimming-costume.

Ross grabbed her hand when she returned and dragged her off before she could change her mind. He was right, the water was quite tolerable after the initial breath-stopping plunge. They romped about in the water, splashing each other and racing each other to a little island that sat in the loch, like a couple of children. Ross always won, for he was a much stronger swimmer than Vicky, but she didn't care. It was great fun and a perfect way to spend her last day of the holidays.

They towelled themselves, but didn't bother to dress. The sun was really very warm. Then they sat on a shared towel and ate their lunch. After lunch Ross stretched himself out and closed his eyes. Vicky followed suit and dozed off and all was silent for some time. Then Vicky awoke, feeling stiff and slightly shivery. She sat up and looked down at Ross, who still slept. She allowed herself the luxury of letting her eyes roam over him. He was really very handsome.

Strong, muscled shoulders and the patch of dark silky hair on his chest. Narrow waist and hips and strong thighs and legs, again with the covering of dark hair. A small smile curved his lips and made his face look strangely young and vulnerable. Vicky felt her heart give an extra surge, with the affection she felt for him. She pulled at a long, feathery grass and chewed at the end of it and pondered on her ambivalent feelings for Ross.

She decided he'd slept long enough and tickled his chest with the feathery end of the grass. He slapped himself, without opening his eyes, obviously thinking it was an insect

121

tickling him. Vicky repeated the procedure, but a little lower, and his eyes flew open. She was leaning over him, laughing down at him, and he muttered, 'Minx,' and grabbed her.

Vicky could never be sure afterwards how it happened, but the next minute she was lying against him, her half-open mouth very near to his. She watched, fascinated, as his grey eyes darkened, and then they were kissing. She couldn't have said whether it was she or he who had closed the gap between them, she only knew that she had never experienced anything like the feelings that surged through her and, as the kiss deepened, she wanted it to go on and on.

Then somehow Ross had rolled her over and he was on top and she could feel every inch of his hard, exciting male body.

Vicky suddenly became aware that Ross had stiffened and pulled his mouth away from hers. She opened her eyes as a voice she knew only too well reached her ears, and then closed them again in anguish as she saw Alison silhouetted against the blue of the sky.

'Well, well, Ross. Incest is it now?' Not a pretty sight.' Her voice was harsh and condemning.

Vicky felt hot shame wash over her in a great tide. What had been a beautiful experience had suddenly turned into something grubby and disgusting. How could she have let herself kiss her own brother like that. She struggled to her feet and grabbed her towel and clothes. She heard Ross say. 'What brings you here, Alison. You don't usually come to the Hall on a Sunday.' His voice was harsh.

'Perhaps it's just as well I did, darling, to save you from yourself. There's no knowing what might have happened if I hadn't interrupted you,' she said mockingly.

Vicky couldn't bear to stay and listen to any more of Alison's taunts. Without stopping to hear why Alison had turned up at the loch, she started to run back to the Hall, not stopping until she fell on to her bed.

Tears started to stream down her cheeks. Everything was ruined. The lovely comradeship that had grown between Ross and herself would be spoiled. They would never be able to behave normally with each other again, she thought. How could she have let herself fall into such a trap. Her feelings weren't the sort of feelings one should have towards a brother. What sort of girl was she? Immoral, wicked! She berated and castigated herself.

When she had spent most of her emotion in tears and only a dull, hopeless misery remained, she got up and showered. She heard someone knocking on her door and slipped into a terry robe and shouted, 'Who is it?' panic-stricken in case it was Ross.

'It's Mrs Thompson. Are you all right, Miss

Vicky? We got worried when you didn't come down to dinner.' She sounded anxious.

'I don't want any dinner, thank you. I don't feel very well,' Vicky said frantically, not wanting anyone to see her.

Too late; the door opened and the worried face of Mrs Thompson peered round it. 'It'll be all that sun and swimming in the loch. Not right at this time of the year. Master Ross doesn't seem well, either. He's just played around with his food.'

Colour flared into Vicky's face at the mention of Ross and Mrs Thompson said, 'You get into bed, Miss Vicky, and I'll bring you up a nice light omelette. You need a good night's sleep or you'll be in no fit state to go off to college tomorrow.'

As far as Vicky was concerned the only bright spot was that she *was* going off to college on the morrow. At least she wouldn't be forced to see Ross and have to pretend that nothing had happened. She lay in bed, curled up into a ball of misery. There was a tap at the door and, thinking it was Mrs Thompson, she called 'Come in.'

The door opened, but it was Ross who stood there, a tray in his hands. Vicky's face reddened, then paled, and her breath came out in a gasp. She clutched the bedclothes up to her chin.

His face looked grim and his eyes were veiled with misery, but a rueful smile twisted his lips at her gesture. 'It's all right, Vicky, I'm not going to attack you. I promise I won't touch you again, but I think we ought to talk.'

He walked over to the bed and placed the tray on her knees. 'Eat your omelette before it gets cold.' He went over to the window and stood with his back to her, stiff and silent.

Vicky struggled to get some of the food down, but it felt as if there was a great lump in her throat and it seemed as if every mouthful might choke her. She laid down her knife and fork eventually, with half of the omelette unfinished, unable to eat any more.

Ross turned and looked at her with brooding, storm-grey eyes. 'I'm sorry about what happened this afternoon. I'm not quite sure how it happened. I can only plead that you are a very attractive young lady and having known you only a short time, I suppose my feelings aren't entirely fraternal towards you. I promise nothing like that will ever happen again.'

Vicky looked down at her clenched hands, unable to meet his eyes and mumbled, 'Don't blame yourself entirely. I didn't exactly put up a fight, did I?'

'That's as maybe, but you're just eighteen and I'm twelve years your senior. I should be able to control my baser instincts by now and I am, after all, your guardian, which makes the whole business even more sordid.'

Vicky felt even more depressed at his words.

So he thought the incident was sordid, did he? The realisation that he had succumbed to a moment of unthinking sexual attraction, that he now bitterly regretted, did nothing to ease her feelings towards him. What bothered her most was the knowledge that if the same circumstances happened again, she would probably respond to him in exactly the same way.

He tried a small smile on her and said, 'Don't feel bad about it. Just forget it ever happened. You have your years at college to look forward to. You'll be bound to meet attractive young men of your own age. Enjoy yourself. I'll see you in the morning. Goodnight, Vicky. Sleep well.'

He left the room swiftly, before Vicky could reply, leaving her staring at the door, with tear-filled eyes.

She realised with pain that in addition to the dark secret that surrounded her father, she now had her own dark secret. She loved her half-brother in a manner that was wrong and unnatural.

CHAPTER EIGHT

Vicky passed a restless night, lying awake for hours, before falling into a troubled, dream-laden sleep. At one point she awoke, damp

126

with perspiration, from a dream in which she heard again the voice of Alison screaming derogatory remarks at her and pointing an accusatory finger.

She was glad when the morning arrived, even though she did feel unrested and edgy. She remembered with alarm that Ross was supposed to be driving with her to Lancaster. He had said he didn't feel she had had enough driving experience to drive that distance by herself. Now she wondered how she could persuade him otherwise. She had no desire to be alone with him for that length of time, not with the strained atmosphere that now existed between them.

She need not have worried however, for Ross apparently felt the same way. At breakfast, when she started to say she would drive herself to Lancaster, he interrupted brusquely and said, 'That will not be necessary. I've arranged for Grainger to drive with you. I'll drive my own car and then we shall have the means to get back without my having to bother with the train. In any case, I don't think the back of your car will take all your luggage. This way I can take some of it.'

Vicky should have felt relieved; perversely, she only felt more hopeless. Obviously, in spite of Ross telling her to forget the incident, he couldn't dismiss it from his mind and behave normally, either, for his manner was cool and very formal, not at all the way they had been before the fateful kiss.

The journey was uneventful. Grainger was the man who looked after all the estate vehicles and he shared the driving with Vicky, to give her experience, chatting to her easily and giving her useful tips.

When they arrived in Lancaster and found the hall of residence, Vicky discovered that she was sharing a room with another girl, much her own age. This was to prove Vicky's salvation from her present low spirits.

Katherine Fellows, or Katie, as she blithely told them to call her, was a small, bubbly, character with short blonde curls that made her look like a Botticelli cherub. In reality she was full of fun, with a wicked sense of humour, but very down-to-earth and staunchly supportive to her friends. Vicky introduced her to Ross and under her sparkling influence he seemed to relax and become more his old self. He didn't linger though, only long enough to see Vicky settled, extracting a promise from her before he went that she would telephone each week to let them know she was all right.

After he'd gone Katie turned bright brown eyes on Vicky and said, 'He's a dish. Is he related to you, you didn't say?'

'My half-brother,' replied Vicky rather shortly, not wanting to go into the details of their relationship at that precise moment.

Katie, as if sensing this and being wise enough not to press for information so early in

128

their friendship, changed the subject to herself and said, 'I have a brother. He brought me here, too, but we don't live as far away as you. Only in the Lake District, near Kendal. We have a pottery there. Kevin runs it now. My father died suddenly last year and Kevin, poor love, had only just left college, but he had to take over the business and look after Mum and me.'

The realisation that Katie had experienced a similar grief to her own encouraged Vicky to talk and she found herself confiding in Katie how her parents had died and she had been taken under Ross's wing and gone to live in Scotland.

A warm friendship developed between the two girls. Katie was doing the same course as Vicky, but specialising in pottery design, whereas Vicky's main subject was painting.

She telephoned Ross each week and they exchanged news. With distance between them, and no physical contact, they managed fairly normal conversation. She also took to writing a letter each week to Sir Malcolm, full of chatty news of her doings at college. Ross informed her that his grandfather eagerly awaited her letters and re-read them several times.

At the end of the first month at college, Katie announced that she was going home for the weekend and then added, 'How would you like to come, too? I've told Mum all about you

129

and she'd love to meet you.'

Vicky looked uncertain and said, 'Are you sure?' She realised that it was no great distance for Katie to travel; she hadn't a car and didn't drive, but she had said it was quite easy to get from Lancaster to Kendal by bus. Vicky thought it was too far for her to nip back and forth to Perthshire, even if things had been normal between her and Ross. At present she wasn't ready to see him again, she still had to grow a protective layer. But this weekend would be flat and lonely without Katie. Although they had made friends with several other students, they tended to do things together, particularly at weekends.

'Of course I'm sure. Do come, it will be such fun. Kevin says there's a dance on Saturday at the village hall. It's only a local "hop" but it's usually good for a laugh,' Katie urged eagerly.

'Well all right, if you're sure. We can go in my car, as long as you act as navigator. I'm not too good yet at driving and finding roads at the same time.' Vicky smiled ruefully.

'Brilliant. I'll go and phone Mum and tell her we'll be arriving on Friday evening,' and Katie loped off.

They started off immediately after their last lecture on the Friday afternoon, but the November light had gone and it was dark by the time they arrived at the Fellows' pottery.

It had previously been a farm and Vicky got a brief impression of a square, solid building in

130

Westmorland stone, built some century and a half earlier. The stone barns had been converted and now served as workshops and store, and sales rooms for the distinctive pottery. It was open to the public and for a small fee visitors could watch the pottery being made, painted and glazed, Katie had told her.

As soon as Vicky drove the car into the gravelled driveway, the door of the house opened and warm light spilled out, illuminating the figure of Katie's mother as she rushed out to greet them. She was a plumper edition of Katie, with the same bright brown eyes and blonde hair, now slightly faded.

She hugged Katie and then Vicky, chattering all the while they unloaded their luggage and carried it into the warm, welcoming kitchen. It was a large, old-fashioned room with a huge range that spilled heat out to tempt the chilled traveller. Delicious smells of baking and a savoury casserole met Vicky's nostrils and made her mouth water. The table was already set and Mrs Fellows said, 'You must be starving. Take Vicky up to the bathroom, Katie, and when you've washed your hands, come straight down and eat. You can unpack afterwards.'

'Where's Kev?' asked Katie.

'Catching up on some paper work in the office. I'll shout him now and then we can all eat together,' Mrs Fellows said.

When Vicky and Katie returned to the

kitchen, Katie's brother was sitting at the table. 'Kev, old thing, how are you?' Katie shouted and rushed over to hug her brother.

Obviously a very real affection existed between them. Katie pulled him to his feet and dragged him over to where Vicky was standing and said gleefully, 'This is my friend, Vicky, Kev.'

A slow smile lit Kevin's face. He had the same warm brown eyes and blond curly hair as his sister and mother, but he was taller and slimmer and his face was more serious. Vicky was to discover that whereas Katie was a complete extrovert, Kevin was quiet and rather shy.

'Hello, it's nice to meet you.' His handclasp was warm and firm and Vicky caught. the brief admiring look that rippled across his face and was warmed by it. It was nice to feel male admiration. It was balm to her bruised spirit.

The weekend was a great success and was only the first of many such visits. Vicky liked Kevin and she soon realised that his feelings for her were deepening each time they met. She told herself if she could just transfer her affection from Ross to Kevin it would solve all her problems. Unfortunately the heart does not always behave in a sensible fashion.

On one visit when she and Kevin had been out to dinner together, he kissed her, with a passion that surprised her. She had thought him cool and reserved. She tried to respond, but eventually he withdrew and looked sadly at her. 'You don't feel that way about me, do you? I'd hoped you were falling in love with me, the way I am with you.'

'I'm sorry, Kevin, I wish I could. I've tried. I like you such a lot,' Vicky said brokenly, upset that she was hurting him and distressed that she could not respond as she would have liked.

'There's someone else, isn't there?' he asked.

She nodded, tears clogging her throat and then she said bitterly, 'But it's all wrong and I can never have him, so I have to get over it.'

'I see,' he said thoughtfully. Vicky thought, 'You don't really, but I can't tell you.' She thought he probably presumed that she was in love with a married man.

'I shall go on hoping, then, if you're sure nothing can come of this love of yours. Maybe you'll grow to love me in time,' Kevin said.

Vicky kissed his cheek affectionately and said, 'Oh I do hope so, but Kevin, don't waste yourself waiting for me. If you meet someone else you can love, grab her. You deserve someone who loves you completely.'

She had gone back to Drumorchy Hall for Christmas and the New Year at Ross's request, but it was not a great success. She and Ross seemed to spend their time circling warily round each other, being studiously polite, afraid to be natural in case their guards slipped. It was a great strain and she was

133

relieved when she could take her leave and spend the remainder of the Christmas vacation at the Fellows' home.

This became the pattern of things over the next three years. She spent as little time as she could at the Hall. Each time she went she told herself that perhaps this time she would find she no longer loved Ross, but her hopes were in vain. She had only to look at him and her heart would behave in its customary crazy fashion and her fingers would itch to touch him; to smooth away the tense lines that were beginning to be etched on his face.

During her first summer vacation, she invited Katie and Kevin to visit the Hall and they accepted. Kevin said he could only spare ten days away from the pottery, but Katie was quite happy to stay longer. An easy friendship developed between Ross and Katie and they laughed and joked together in a manner that left Vicky feeling envious. She wished she could recapture the old comradeship that had once existed between Ross and herself. Then she realised that there had never been the carefree friendship between them that had grown between him and Katie. They were more like elder brother and sister than she and Ross had ever been.

Towards the end of Kevin's stay, Ross suddenly said, 'He's in love with you, isn't he? Are you going to marry him? You'll have to ask my permission, you know, you're still officially my ward.' The words were said with unusual harshness.

'Yes, I think he is, but I don't know how I feel about him.' Vicky wasn't about to tell him the truth about her feelings for Kevin. 'I don't think I'm ready for marriage yet, so you don't have to worry on that score. Although perhaps you'd be relieved to get me off your hands,' Vicky concluded in a rush.

'Damn you, Vicky, you know that's not true and if you don't know how you feel about him, then you don't love him enough to marry him.' He left the subject at that. Vicky could have told him that she already knew she didn't love Kevin enough to marry him. How could she when her heart was already given elsewhere.

She thoroughly enjoyed her college course and with the high assessments she had received for her assignments, she knew she would pass her exams and get her diploma.

Eventually Kevin realised that the situation between them was not going to change and he started seeing less of Vicky and more of the daughter of a local farmer. Vicky was pleased for him. She liked Rachel and thought she would make Kevin a good wife.

Katie was upset and bewailed the fact that she had hoped to have Vicky as a sister-in-law, but Vicky explained that it was her fault, not Kevin's, that nothing had come of their friendship.

'I don't know about you. You've had the

opportunity to become something special to several nice fellas, but you remain aloof. It's my belief you've got a secret lover somewhere,' Katie teased.

Vicky's face flamed at her words and Katie looked surprised at Vicky's reaction. 'Don't talk such utter rot, Katie. Of course I haven't got a secret lover. I hardly have the time, do I; we're very rarely away from each other,' Vicky said vehemently.

As her twenty-first birthday approached, Vicky wondered how Ross would mark it and whether he would formally relinquish his guardianship.

Her curiosity was ended by a telephone call from Ross. Vicky's pulse quickened at the low, attractive voice as he said, 'I'm planning a dinner party for your birthday, Vicky. You will be able to get home for the weekend, won't you?'

'Yes, I expect so, but I shall have to return to college on the Monday, I have an exam later that week.'

Vicky was showered with gifts by all her friends at Drumorchy, but the gift that took her breath away with its beauty was Ross's. It was a diamond and sapphire necklace. Vicky had stammered her thanks, wondering what had possessed him to buy such an obviously expensive gift.

The dinner party was pleasant. Vicky remembered the barbecue they'd had for her eighteenth birthday. She wondered where the girl of three years ago had gone; she felt a mature woman now, with all the problems maturity brought with it. Ross made a little speech, in which he relinquished his role of guardian.

She had seen nothing of Alison until the Monday morning, just before she was due to return to Lancaster. She was putting her suitcase in the boot of the car when Alison sauntered over to her.

'So you've officially come of age; perhaps Ross can have a life of his own now. If you've got any decency you'll stay away and make a life for yourself elsewhere. You've been nothing but trouble to him. I don't know what you do to him, but after every visit you make he's strained and miserable.'

Vicky stared at Alison askance, hardly able to comprehend her meaning. Was it true? Had she been a burden to Ross? Did her visits upset him? And if so, why? After all it was at his insistence that she made the visits.

Suddenly a flood of temper ran through Vicky like a hot tide. She remembered all the barbs she had suffered from Alison's vicious tongue over the years and her comment at the start of their acquaintance about how she intended to marry Ross. Her voice sounded high and thin in her own ears as she said, 'Oh, you can have a clear field to try and ensnare him, if that's what you want, but I feel I must

137

point out that if you haven't managed to trap him during the past three years I can hardly see you doing so now.'

Alison's hand shot out and contacted with Vicky's cheek in a resounding slap. 'You little slut. Don't think I don't know you've tried to keep him dancing to your tune. I haven't forgotten what I saw that day before you went away to college, you know.'

Vicky banged the boot shut with a thud. Her eyes were blinded with tears and her face stung from the slap. She walked quickly away. Somehow she had to compose herself before she said her goodbyes to Ross. She went to her room and tried to repair the ravages to her face. The red marks of Alison's fingers were still clearly etched on her cheek and she splashed her face with cold water and applied a tinted foundation to try to disguise them.

She found Ross and told him she was about to depart. He looked hard at her face and said, 'What have you done to your cheek?' touching it with a long forefinger.

'I banged it on the car when I was putting my case in.' The gentleness of his touch caused the tears to start again.

He looked concerned and said, 'Are you sure you're all right, Vicky love?'

'I'm fine. I'll be off now,' she murmured, with a catch in her voice.

He bent and touched her forehead with a featherlight kiss. 'Take care. Drive carefully.'

Vicky threw herself into her exams, thinking work was probably the panacea for some of her problems. Ross had mentioned on the night of her birthday dinner, that she would be coming back to stay for good when her course was completed. She hadn't contradicted him at the time, but she knew for certain now that she couldn't go back to live permanently at Drumorchy.

She contemplated asking for the house in Cornwall to be vacated and going to live and paint there, but she had severed all her connections there now. Then Katie made a proposition to her. She said she and her mother had talked it over and now that Kevin was getting married and moving out of the family home, how would Vicky like to come and live with them and paint in the Lake District.

Vicky thought it over and decided that might be the answer to her dilemma. She accepted gratefully, then thought ruefully that she had to break the news to Ross.

She finished her exams and rang Ross to tell him that she had passed them. He said, 'Well, how soon before you come back to set up your studio here? I've arranged for one end of the shop to be devoted to displaying your paintings.'

Vicky gulped and plunged in. 'Ross, I'm not coming back to Drumorchy to live permanently.'

CHAPTER NINE

There was a long, awkward silence and then Ross's voice, ragged and incredulous, vibrated over the line. 'Did I mishear, or did you really say you weren't coming back to Drumorchy to live?'

Vicky swallowed and tried to make her voice sound normal, but it still came out shaky and breathlessly nervous. 'You didn't mishear. I was going to explain that Katie and her mother have invited me to live with them, now that Kevin is getting married and will have his own home. There's a barn I can convert to a studio and when visitors come to the pottery I shall be able to interest them in my pictures.'

'Wasn't the studio I gave you good enough, or the visitors to the Hall suitable purchasers of your pictures?' Or perhaps the Scottish scenery doesn't inspire you as much as the Lakes?' Ross's voice was laced with sarcasm and anger in equal proportions.

Vicky felt dreadful. She couldn't possibly explain the real reason why she couldn't live at the Hall permanently. She floundered along, trying to soothe Ross's obviously injured feelings. 'Ross, please. Don't be like this. It's nothing to do with the Hall. You know how I love it and the Scottish countryside. It's just that Katie and I are such good friends and I haven't any really close friends in Scotland. Do try to understand.'

'I'm damned if I can understand. You say you have no friends here. What about me and all the other folk who always go out of their way to welcome you and invite you to their homes when you're here for visits? What about grandfather? He's been so looking forward to having you around.' His voice, which had been hard and angry when he started his speech, had softened and sounded husky by the end, and that made Vicky feel worse.

She hesitated and said, 'Ross, please don't crowd me. I do have my reasons for doing this. Please bear with me.'

'I thought at one time that you might be contemplating marrying Kevin, as you know, but then nothing came of it and he met someone else, so we naturally presumed you'd be returning when you'd completed your course.' He paused and then continued coaxingly, 'Vicky, I don't want to pressure you, but will you, at least, come back for a visit before you take up residence with the Fellows? You see grandfather isn't at all well. He's had another stroke. I really don't know how much longer he will last. Won't you come and stay for a while for his sake? We haven't seen much of you for some months, apart from the short visit for your birthday.'

Vicky faltered and weakened, whilst muttering under her breath, 'And that was hardly a roaring success,' referring to her birthday visit and the row with Alison.

'Sorry, I didn't hear what you said,' Ross chipped in.

'Oh nothing. All right. I'll come and stay as long as you think I can be of any help with grandfather,' Vicky said resignedly.

'Thanks, love. He'll be so thrilled,' Ross said warmly. 'When shall we expect you?'

'At the weekend. I've got to clear my property out of my room at college,' Vicky said shortly, wondering how she had been manoeuvred into capitulating.

'Drive carefully. We'll look forward to having you home again. 'Bye.' Ross said sweetly. Vicky wondered whether she was imagining the slightly triumphant note in his voice.

No matter how much she told herself she was being foolish, Vicky couldn't suppress a thrill of pleasure and anticipation as she drove through the huge wrought-iron gates and up the long drive to Drumorchy Hall. The sight of the beautiful architecture never failed to move her.

She remembered the angry words she and Alison had exchanged on her last visit and wondered how they could avoid another confrontation. That was one person who wouldn't be pleased to see her, she thought ruefully. She consoled herself with the thought that Alison and the visitors would have gone home by now, for it was almost six-thirty, and a blissful Sabbath stretched before her before she would have to see Alison.

She dumped a couple of her suitcases in the entrance hall and went in search of Mrs Thompson; Thompson would probably fetch the rest of her luggage out of the car for her. She poked her head round the kitchen door and said gaily, 'Hello there, I can smell something good.'

Mrs Thompson turned from the stove, a welcoming smile on her face. 'Miss Vicky, how lovely to see you again.' Mrs Thompson opened her arms and Vicky ran into them, to be hugged firmly. 'Ye'll be back for good now, then? That will aye be nice.'

Vicky didn't reply directly to the question. Obviously Ross had not mentioned her plans and there didn't seem much point in spoiling Mrs Thompson's obvious pleasure at this moment. Time enough when she left the Hall for good.

'Is your husband busy? Could he unload my car for me, while I clean up?' she asked.

'Of course. He'll be pleased to do that for you.'

'Where's Ross?' Vicky asked.

'I think he's gone up to see Sir Malcolm. He usually does, after the visitors have gone,' replied Mrs Thompson.

'How is Sir Malcolm?' Vicky enquired anxiously.

'Very frail. This last stroke knocked him about, I'm afraid,' Mrs Thompson replied sadly.

'I'll go up to his room and see how he is.'

Vicky tapped gently on the door of Sir Malcolm's sitting-room and Ross opened it.

She watched his eyes lighten and felt the old familiar longing coursing through her veins.

'Vicky, love! We never heard you arrive,' said Ross and stretched out his hands as if to embrace her; then, as if thinking better of it, he let them fall to his sides.

Vicky tore her eyes reluctantly from Ross and directed them towards Sir Malcolm. She was shocked by his changed appearance. In the month since she had last seen him, he seemed to have shrunk visibly and his skin was like old parchment, stretched, as if too tightly, over his facial bones. He was sitting in his wheelchair, a plaid shawl covering his knees, and she ran over to him and dropped on to her knees beside his chair. She caught his hand and held it to her cheek.

'Grandfather, how are you?' she asked huskily, realising how very fond she had grown of the crusty old man over the years.

'Better for seeing you,' he managed and Vicky saw tears in his faded blue eyes. He stroked her bright hair with his mobile hand. 'You've come back to stay with us now, haven't you?' he said in his faltering voice. Vicky caught a warning glance from Ross and said nothing to disaffirm his belief.

She chatted to him for a few minutes longer and then said, 'I'm going to have a shower and change. I'll see you at dinner, shall I?'

'I'll see how I feel. I don't get down too often for dinner now, I'm afraid, but we'll see if we can manage it for your first night back.' His voice had grown faint and weary by the end of the sentence.

Ross followed her out of the room and she turned concerned eyes to him. 'He's grown dreadfully frail since I last saw him.'

'That's what I told you. You won't say anything to him about your plans to leave, will you? It would upset him too much,' Ross said, his eyes narrowed, as if not sure what her response would be.

'No, of course not. I wouldn't upset him for the world,' Vicky said indignantly.

'You might not have to curtail your plans for too long,' Ross said harshly.

'What do you mean by that,' Vicky asked, upset at his tone.

'The doctor says another stroke will probably finish him. His heart is very weak,' Ross replied bleakly.

A sadness filled Vicky at his words. She had never expected to grow so fond of Sir Malcolm, but she had and she would miss him.

Sunday was wet and cold and Vicky spent much of her day sorting through her possessions, those that she had left at the Hall from previous visits and those that she had just brought with her. She unpacked all her painting materials and arranged them in the studio, admitting to herself that she would enjoy working there. She played chess with Sir Malcolm until he grew too tired to concentrate, then read to him for a while, but she soon realised how very quickly he tired now. She and Ross spent the evening together watching an old film on television. They talked very little, but the silence was not an uncomfortable one and Vicky began to hope that she and Ross could work out some formula for being at ease with one another again.

After breakfast on the Monday morning, she was about to make herself scarce by going to the studio before Alison arrived, when the dining-room door opened and a plump, cheerful face, capped with a mop of riotous grey curls, appeared round the door and a cheerful Scottish voice said, 'Good morning, Master Ross. I'm here; what have we got on the agenda today.' A pair of bright brown eyes twinkled at Vicky and the lady continued, 'You must be Miss Vicky. I've heard all about you.'

Vicky's mouth dropped open and it was several moments before she found her voice. 'H-hello. I'm sorry I don't think I know who you are.'

Ross grinned. 'This is Mary McNaughton, my new assistant. I'd forgotten you didn't

146

know about her.'

Vicky stood there gasping like a landed fish, feeling utterly astounded and then, eventually, managed, 'I'm delighted to meet you.' And she was, too.

Mary went off, waving cheerfully. 'I expect I'll see you later, Vicky.'

Vicky turned quickly, blocking Ross's path, as he went to follow Mary, and hissed, 'What happened to Alison? When did she leave? You kept that very quiet.'

'Aren't you pleased? You never really got on with her, did you?' he queried, with a lift of his eyebrow, and then added, 'We had a difference of opinion and she saw a job offered in London as PA to a top businessman, that suited her ambitions better. I think she realised that she wasn't going to attain the status she desired here.' This was said smoothly, but Vicky detected the hidden meaning behind the words. She gathered that Alison had finally realised that Ross had no intention of marrying her and a great wave of joy and relief washed over her. She wondered what the disagreement had been over, but decided not to pry at this stage. Instead she smiled a wide smile and said, 'I'm absolutely delighted. I'm afraid Alison and I would never have been compatible no matter how long we knew each other.'

Ross grinned. 'Yes, I can appreciate that.'

Vicky settled into a pleasant routine at

Drumorchy Hall. She painted, helped with the visitors or in the shop, where a corner had been turned over entirely to her paintings, spent as much time as possible with Sir Malcolm before he tired, and renewed her friendships with the local people. Only two things marred her happiness in any way. The first was that Sir Malcolm seemed to fade a little each day and the other was that, although she and Ross seemed to have resumed a friendly companionship, Vicky knew that it was a very brittle arrangement and full of weaknesses. She couldn't kill her feelings for him. She had only to look at him and her pulse would quicken and if he accidentally touched her, shivers of excitement would ripple through her blood.

She realised with dismay that she had spent three years avoiding him in an endeavour to expurgate the attraction he had for her and she might as well not have bothered. Nothing had really changed.

The weeks went by and without Alison around they were some of the most pleasant Vicky had spent. Mary McNaughton was an absolute dear and a happy friendship had developed between her and Vicky.

She had not needed to quiz Ross about the reason for his and Alison's row, Mrs Thompson had been only too eager to tell her. She told Vicky that Mr Thompson had witnessed the argument between herself and

148

Alison and the slap that Alison had administered and decided that it was his duty to tell Ross what had upset Vicky before her departure, when Ross had commented on the fact that Vicky seemed upset. Ross had been furious and had confronted Alison. Mrs Thompson said that they hadn't heard all the details, but he and Alison had had quite a row, with voices raised, and the outcome was that he had told Alison to look for another situation.

Vicky kept in touch with Katie and was keeping open the option to join Katie and her mother at the pottery. She had explained about Sir Malcolm's failing health and his desire to have her at the Hall and Katie had understood.

Then towards the end of August Sir Malcolm gently slipped away. He had been particularly tired and had stayed in bed, but had asked Vicky to read to him after dinner. Ross was doing some work in his study. She had been reading for some twenty minutes when she detected a change in Sir Malcolm's breathing. He seemed to be struggling to get air into his lungs.

'Are you all right, grandfather?' she had asked anxiously and propped him up a little higher on his pillows.

'Pain—here,' he gasped, placing a thin, veined hand on his chest.

'I'll run and get Ross,' she said quickly.

'No—no time. Come—closer,' he struggled to say.

Vicky leaned nearer to him, her anxious blue eyes seeking his. 'Don't try to talk. Rest,' she urged.

'Must—have to—tell you. You're a dear—girl. I've—grown to love you—very much. You've—more than—atoned.' He gave one last painful gasp and closed his eyes.

Vicky laid her ear to his chest and tried to find a heartbeat, but she knew he had gone.

She rushed to Ross's study, tears trickling down her cheeks. 'Ross, it's grandfather!' she gasped urgently.

'Is he ill?' asked Ross, getting swiftly to his feet.

'I think he's dead, Ross.'

They made their way back together and Ross bent over his grandfather and then straightened up and Vicky watched as his face contorted with emotion. She put her arms around him and held him tight for some minutes.

Sir Malcolm was laid to rest in the family vault with his beloved wife and daughter. The Hall had been closed to visitors and seemed strangely quiet. Vicky didn't know quite what to do with herself. She couldn't paint, her inspiration seemed to have deserted her. Ross seemed to spend most of his time in the study.

A few days after the funeral, Ross informed her at breakfast that the family solicitor would be coming to read his grandfather's will.

'You won't need me there, will you?' she asked.

'I think so, yes,' he replied.

Vicky was surprised, but didn't argue, and she went with Ross to the drawing-room when the solicitor's arrival was announced.

The Thompsons and other old retainers were present, for there were bequests of money and gifts for all of them. Then the solicitor turned to Vicky and to her great surprise informed her that Sir Malcolm had left her all his wife's jewellery and some books that she had often read and admired. The jewellery was very valuable and Vicky felt quite overwhelmed.

As they had expected, the bulk of Sir Malcolm's money went to Ross. The estate, of course, had already been made over to him some years before.

Vicky thought that everything was over, when the solicitor suddenly handed a sealed envelope over to Ross and said, 'This was given into my keeping at the time of your mother's death, with the strict instruction that it was only to be handed to you after Sir Malcolm's death, providing that you were an adult. It has been in my possession for thirty-three years now and I have no notion what it contains. I expect you will wish to be alone to read it, so I will take my leave now. Should you need any advice, please don't hesitate to contact me.'

Ross looked stunned, but saw the solicitor out, then went to his study. Vicky guessed he wanted to be by himself when he read the letter from his mother.

Mrs Thompson had gone back into the kitchen and Vicky joined her there to get her to make some coffee for them both. She thought Ross might like some, but decided to give him some time to digest his letter and then she would take him some. She sat at the kitchen table chatting to Mrs Thompson, when she suddenly heard Ross calling her.

She hurried to the study to find Ross seated at the desk, his face pale and tense, the pages of the letter scattered in front of him. He picked the sheets of paper up, with fingers that shook, and held them out to her. 'Read it!' he said huskily.

'Are you sure you want me to?' Vicky asked awkwardly.

'I think you should. It affects you indirectly.'

As she read the closely-written sheets, it was almost as if Helen was there, telling her story. She wrote how she had met and fallen in love with a man twice her own age, Sir Miles Latimer, when he was visiting Kirriemuir Castle. He was married, with two teenage daughters.

'There was no way he could leave his family and get a divorce,' she wrote. 'You see he is an important man—a Member of Parliament—in fact, a Cabinet Minister. He is ambitious, and a divorce and a scandal like this would ruin his career, so I knew all along that there was no future for us, but that didn't stop us loving blindly. We meet at the little bothy on the hill whenever we can. I am obsessed with him. I cannot bear to be apart from him.'

She went on to tell how eventually Sir Miles had said they must stop meeting, then she went on to say how a young man had come to do her sculpture and fallen in love with her. She told how she had decided to marry the young man, John Tremayne, in the hope that she could make some sort of life without Sir Miles.

Then the letter went on, in stark tragedy, to tell how she couldn't bring herself to let John make love to her and how she had then discovered that she was expecting Sir Miles' child and been forced to tell John the truth. She said that John had been bitterly hurt but had offered to stand by her, if she could promise him that there was some hope that she would learn to love him, but she could offer no such hope. She explained how John had eventually left her and then how depressed she had become after the birth of Ross.

She wrote, 'I have been weak and foolish. I have cheated a good man and I cannot tell my father the truth, for he believes me blameless and idolises me. I cannot live with myself, I

153

must end it all. Forgive me, my beloved son. I entrust you to my father's care for I am sure he will make a better job of raising you than I could ever have done. Try not to condemn me. I can only plead that I did not love wisely, but too well.'

Vicky could barely comprehend what she was reading. So Ross was not her father's child at all, that was the reason her father had behaved as he had. But even so greatly wronged, he had not disclosed the truth to Sir Malcolm, so that Helen's reputation should not be besmirched in her father's eyes.

Then the full implication hit her and a feeling of undiluted joy and the sensation that a great burden she had been carrying had suddenly slipped from her shoulders, washed over her. Ross was not her brother. There was nothing wrong with her love for him. Even if he never reciprocated, she need never again feel ashamed of her feelings for him.

She said nothing of her realisation, the fact didn't appear to have registered with Ross. He just sat, his hands clenched and his face a mask, as if unable to take it in.

She touched his shoulder gently. 'I'm going to get you a drink and then we'll talk.' She poured brandy into two glasses, handed one to him and sipped the other herself, then she went and collected the coffee. When she returned he had drunk the brandy and there was a little more colour in his face.

She poured a cup of coffee and handed it to him. She said firmly, 'What are you going to do about it?'

He looked at her for a moment as if weighing up the question and then said, 'Find out about this Sir Miles Latimer and then go and see him. After all he is my father. But how could she have done it?' he asked in a bewildered voice.

Vicky thought he meant how could his mother have fallen in love with a married man and thought, 'Quite easily. We don't always fall in love with suitable people.' But he continued, 'How could she have taken her own life and gone to her grave without revealing the truth? All these years I've lived with bitterness towards a man who had been so grievously wronged. How could she have let her own father condemn someone and hate him, rather than tell him the truth about herself?'

Vicky said gently, 'Ross, don't condemn her. You can't really know how she felt. She was weak, yes, but I don't believe she was deliberately cruel. Just imagine, too, how much courage it must have taken to keep quiet about her pregnancy rather than ruin his career. I think she was misguided, but I think she was a poor, unhappy girl and deserves our sympathy.'

'I expect you're right and I shall come to terms with it. It's just that it's such a shock. I think I'll ring the solicitor and tell him the

155

contents of the letter and ask his advice about what I should do.'

'I'm sure that's the sensible thing to do.' She stood on tiptoe and touched a gentle, loving kiss to his cheek. 'Everything will work out for you, I feel certain, Ross.'

'Bless you, Vicky, and thanks for being here,' he said huskily.

Two days later Ross said, 'He wants to meet me—my father, I mean.'

Vicky's eyes widened. 'What happened, then?'

'The solicitor got in touch with him. His wife is dead now and his two daughters are married with children of their own, and living abroad. He has retired from public life.'

'Where does he live? Are you going to see him?'

'He lives in the south—Surrey—and yes, I'm going to visit him. I have to find out what he's like for my own peace of mind.'

'I can understand that. When will you go?' Vicky asked.

'At the end of the week. He's invited me to stay for a few days.' Ross looked at her and their suddenly blurted out quickly, 'Will you come with me, Vicky?'

Vicky looked surprised. 'Are you sure you want me there? Wouldn't you rather see him on your own?'

'No, I need you there,' said Ross decisively.

'Then, of course, I'll come with you,' Vicky

agreed.

The Hall was still closed and, leaving Mary holding the fort as far as estate matters were concerned, they set off on Thursday, stayed overnight along the way, and eventually arrived at Oakenham House, Sir Miles' home, late Friday afternoon. He was obviously wealthy, for the house and grounds were impressive.

They were shown into a large, comfortable drawing-room by a manservant and then Sir Miles entered. Vicky watched, fascinated, as he walked through the doorway. There was no mistaking the similarities between him and Ross, the walk and the way he held his head. His hair was iron-grey, but had probably been dark like Ross's. He was still a handsome man, although nearing seventy now.

As he walked towards them, she saw his eyes and if she had had any doubts, they would have settled them. The same storm-grey eyes surveyed them. Now she knew why she had never been able to find those eyes amongst Ross's Cameron ancestors, they were inherited from his father.

He stopped before he reached them and said, 'Ross' almost hesitantly and with emotion showing in his face. He held out his hand and Ross took it and Vicky saw the elder man relax visibly. Obviously he had been uncertain of Ross's reaction to the news that he was his father.

Vicky felt his eyes and the curiosity in them, as he turned to her.

Ross said, 'This is Victoria Tremayne, John Tremayne's daughter,' but he made no mention of the fact that until a few days ago they had believed themselves related. He still hadn't mentioned the fact they were not related and if it affected his feelings towards her. The thought took away some of the joy that the discovery had given Vicky. Obviously it made no difference to Ross.

'Please sit and make yourselves comfortable. I'd like to explain to you my feelings for your mother, Ross. I loved her very much and her death pained me greatly. I want you to know that if I had dreamed that she was carrying my child, I would have got a divorce and married her. We met and fell in love. I make no excuses for myself. I was a married man and much older than Helen, I should never have let it happen. My marriage was more a marriage of expediency than love; my wife came from a good family and could help me in my political career. Then I met Helen and realised what I had missed, and my good sense disappeared. I think we both realised nothing could come of it and eventually we agreed to part. I received a letter. I was still staying at Kirriemuir Castle. The letter begged me to meet her again. I went to the bothy where we used to meet, but she didn't turn up and then I heard that she had agreed to marry your father, Victoria. I presumed that she had decided this was the best course of action and I kept out of her life. I heard nothing more of her, until I read of her tragic suicide. I was heartbroken, but never dreamed why she had done it and that her child was also mine. If only she had told me. My career never meant that much to me; in fact after her death it all seemed rather futile and I never did reach the heights I had once aspired to.' Sir Miles stopped talking and looked at Ross.

Ross had said nothing whilst his father had been talking, but Vicky said, 'I found the scorched remains of your letter years ago when I visited the bothy.'

Ross turned astonished eyes to her. 'Why on earth didn't you tell me?'

'I only realised that she had been in the habit of meeting a man there, not who it was or that he was your father. I could see no point in revealing the information and hurting you, when it didn't really alter the situation.'

'But it would have vindicated your father,' Ross said softly, 'and you always wanted to do that when you first came to live at the Hall.'

'Perhaps so, but by the time I found the letter, it didn't seem so important,' Vicky said.

Sir Miles broke in at this point. 'Ross, I don't know how you feel about me, but I'd like to get to know you. You're the son I always wanted and never thought to have.' He sounded wistful. 'You probably don't want me to broadcast the fact that I'm your father, although I'd like to shout it from the rooftops.'

Ross looked surprised at his father's words and said, 'I'm sorry, I'm not prepared to change my name from Cameron. I feel I owe it to my grandfather to retain the family name; he was the only father I knew when I was growing up. But I would like you to make a statement to the effect that I am your son. You see, Vicky and I have spent the last few years thinking we were half-brother and sister and I have to confess that my feelings for her have never been entirely brotherly. In fact having her as a sister was the last relationship I wanted from her.'

Sir Miles smiled and said, 'I shall be delighted to make a statement to the press.'

Vicky felt happiness rush through her in a warm wave. She wanted to sing with joy. She turned glowing eyes towards Ross and started to say something, but he shook his head and she stopped. Dare she hope? Did this mean what she hoped it meant?

Sir Miles rang a bell for someone to show them to their rooms. Before Ross disappeared into his room, she caught at his sleeve and said, 'Ross, what did you mean downstairs about not wanting to be my brother?'

He smiled and dropped a kiss on the end of her nose and said, 'We've waited three years, we can wait a few more days until we get back to Drumorchy.'

So Vicky had to contain her impatience, but, although she enjoyed the weekend with Sir Miles, she was eager to return to Scotland and find out about Ross's feelings for her.

Sir Miles was as good as his word. He gave a press interview and stories appeared about how he had just discovered that Ross was his son. It was a nine days' wonder and then more exciting news nudged it into obscurity. Drumorchy village rocked with the news rather longer, but then fresh news was to set their tongues wagging anew.

They departed on the Monday, having arranged that Sir Miles should come and spend some time at Drumorchy Hall getting to know Ross properly.

The Hall and village were humming with the news when they returned and Mrs Thompson nodded her head sagely and said, 'I always thought there was something funny about Miss Helen's marriage to your father, Vicky. Didn't I hint as much?'

On the Tuesday Vicky barely saw Ross and she hovered between hope and despair, then he suddenly appeared and said, 'Dress yourself up tonight, Vicky. 'We're going out to eat. I think we might have something to celebrate, unless I've badly miscalculated.'

Vicky did as she was bid and dressed herself in a romantic dress of creamy lace and went in search of Ross. He was in his study and said, 'Come here, I can't wait any longer to find out

161

how you feel and you look so delectable I can't keep my hands off you for long.'

He sat her down and stood in front of her, a determined look on his face. 'Vicky, do you remember that day long ago when we kissed? I told you I was sorry and it wouldn't happen again and I made sure it never did. I avoided circumstances like that again, but it wasn't because I didn't want to kiss you. I had fallen in love with you, you see, but I thought it was wrong because of our relationship. I told myself I should marry someone else, but I didn't want to. I though you would find someone and for a time it seemed as if you had when you grew so friendly with Kevin, but you weren't in love with him, were you? Dare I hope that the reason was that your heart was already given to someone else, perhaps to me?'

At his words Vicky could no longer stay in her seat and she jumped up and moved towards him with outstretched arms. She was very soon clasped tightly in his arms and crushed against his chest. Then his lips were on hers, asking and receiving all that they desired.

Ross broke away for a moment to whisper hoarsely, 'Tell me you love me. I've waited so long to hear you say it.'

'I love you, Ross, with all my heart. I think I fell in love with you the first moment I saw you, but I've spent three years trying to kill that love, because I thought it was wicked of me to feel that way.

'You are going to marry me, aren't you?' he asked, kissing her again.

'Try and stop me,' murmured Vicky against his lips.

'Very soon?' His mouth came down again and his arm tightened.

'Whenever you want.' Another kiss.

Vicky suddenly thought that her father and Ross's mother would approve of the union between their children. The old wrong would be cancelled. And as Vicky realised that there were no more dark secrets between them, only a bright future stretching before them, her heart felt as if it had wings.

We hope you have enjoyed this Large Print book. Other Chivers Press or G.K. Hall & Co. Large Print books are available at your library or directly from the publishers.

For more information about current and forthcoming titles, please call or write, without obligation, to:

Chivers Press Limited
Windsor Bridge Road
Bath BA2 3AX
England
Tel. (01225) 335336

OR

G.K. Hall & Co.
P.O. Box 159
Thorndike, Maine 04986
USA
Tel. (800) 223-2336

All our Large Print titles are designed for easy reading, and all our books are made to last.